THE FISHERMAN'S ORPHAN DAUGHTER

VICTORIAN ROMANCE

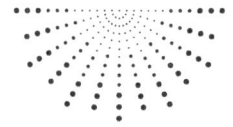

ROSIE SWAN

PUREREAD.COM

Copyright © 2024 PureRead Ltd

www.pureread.com

All rights reserved. No part of this publication may be reproduced, distributed or transmitted in any form or by any means, without prior written permission.

Publisher's Note: This is a work of fiction. Names, characters, places, and incidents are a product of the author's imagination. Locales and public names are sometimes used for atmospheric purposes. Any resemblance to actual people, living or dead, or to businesses, companies, events, institutions, or locales is completely coincidental.

CONTENTS

Chapter 1	1
Chapter 2	10
Chapter 3	15
Chapter 4	22
Chapter 5	28
Chapter 6	35
Chapter 7	43
Chapter 8	49
Chapter 9	54
Chapter 10	63
Chapter 11	68
Chapter 12	76
Chapter 13	83
Chapter 14	89
Chapter 15	96
Chapter 16	104
Chapter 17	110
Chapter 18	116
Chapter 19	123
Chapter 20	128
Chapter 21	134
Chapter 22	141
Love Victorian Romance?	147
Our Gift To You	149

CHAPTER ONE

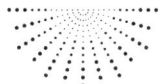

Ambrose Green had a routine to his life, and that was the way he liked things. Every morning, he awoke before dawn and brewed himself a strong coffee before heading out to the docks. He hauled the tarp off his small fishing boat while the sun was just beginning to rise, and he sailed out down the Humber toward the North Sea for a day's catching as soon as his morning checks were complete. If the rain was pouring, as it often was on any day in the East of England, he would pull part of the tarp over his head to keep the rain from bothering him, and he would sit alone in his boat and wait for his nets to fill. Despite his increasing age, the muscles in his arm were dependable and strong, honed by years of hauling his catch aboard alone. Once he had a good catch of fish, he'd turn the boat towards home and sell his catch to the market stall holders before buying a penny bowl of Old Jenny's stew to warm him up and fill his stomach. He went back to his one-room house and was asleep before it was dark, ready to start the entire process again the following morning. The only things that changed over the years were the aches in his back, growing ever more demanding as the years passed, and the people he saw around him, as children were born and grew and elderly neighbours aged and died.

Ambrose Green spoke very little to anyone, and often responded to conversation with a grunt of acknowledgement or, at most, a gruff word or two in reply, but he was still well-respected by those who knew him as a hard worker and a gentle soul. "Poor man," Old Jenny would sometimes say to her other customers, after Ambrose had purchased his daily stew and departed. "His wife died, you know, must be fifteen years back now, not six months after they got married. Childhood sweethearts, they were. But that winter was bad for all of us, and the sickness took her and the little one she was expecting. Don't think he's ever been quite right since."

Ambrose knew what people said about him, but he did not mind overly much. As long as no-one bothered him or interrupted his routine, they could say what they liked. The light had gone out of his life when his dear Peggy died, and although strangers may pity him, he had no want nor need for anyone else in his life. He had spent the past fifteen years following the steady rhythm of his daily routine to help him fight the hollow ache Peggy's death left in his heart, and if tears sometimes stung his eyes as he stared at the coast of England from his fishing boat and thought of her, at least no one else would ever be there to see it.

So when Ambrose woke up one grey and rainy morning in October, fifteen years to the day since his dear Peggy left this earth, he followed his routine like it was any other day. He may have moved a little slower as he dressed, and he stared at his coffee mug for a longer moment than was typical before drinking it, but his routine carried him through the ache he felt as he readied for the day.

He made his way down to the docks in the grimy pre-dawn light, the rain soaking through the worn toe of his boot, and moved to haul the tarp off his boat to begin his preparations for departure. But as he moved to grab the tarp, he noticed a point where it had already been pulled back from the edge, leaving a space just large enough for some wily creature to slither inside. Ambrose let out an annoyed breath. He didn't leave anything valuable in the fishing boat overnight, but if some kids had been playing in it or looking for something to nick, he'd have to have words with the dock master. It wasn't safe to have young things running around near the water at night. And if it was an animal... well, Ambrose just hoped it hadn't curled up to die in there. He could probably sell it for meat and fur at the market if it was anything sizeable, but he'd have to change his plans for the day to do it, and today of all days, Ambrose just wanted things to proceed as intended.

Moving more slowly now, so as not to startle a sleeping creature and earn himself a bite in the process, Ambrose gently pulled the tarp from the top of the boat and peered inside. Raindrops struck the boat's wooden deck. Past the tangle of nets, Ambrose could see a small shape, curled up beneath another, smaller tarp. Ambrose climbed onto the deck and took a careful step towards it. He saw a mass of tangled blonde hair, and he gasped. It was a child.

A small girl, he realised, as he got closer still, curled up in a ball like a kitten on the deck of the ship. Ambrose did not know much about children, but he reckoned this one must be about three years old at most, with pale, dirt-covered skin and freckles peeking out across her nose. She continued to sleep as Ambrose stared at her, shivering slightly under the tarp she was using as a blanket.

Who was she, Ambrose wondered, and what was she doing here? A child that small should not be alone. Surely she had someone who cared for her and was missing her. Had she run away?

The little girl coughed and pulled the tarp tighter around herself. "Hey," Ambrose said softly, his voice rasping from lack of use. "Hey, little one. You alright in there?"

The girl stirred. She sat up slowly, rubbing the sleep from her eyes, and the tarp slid down to reveal a raggedy grey dress and goose pimples down her arms. She blinked and looked at Ambrose, and Ambrose waited for the inevitable shriek of fear that any child would make when finding a heavily bearded stranger staring at her upon waking, but it did not come. She stared at Ambrose with huge green eyes, taking in the details of his appearance, and blinked again.

"Where'd you come from, little one?" Ambrose asked, speaking as softly and kindly as he could. He did not want the child to startle or bolt. "You shouldn't be in there."

The girl blinked at him again.

"You got parents?" Ambrose asked. The girl did not reply. Was she just shy, Ambrose wondered, or could she not speak? He did not know when kids were supposed to be able to talk, but he figured a three year old would be able to say *something*, wouldn't she?

"You alright, Green?" a voice shouted. Jack Hornby, who kept his boat on the dock next to Ambrose's, had noticed the break in Ambrose's routine. He did not know the significance of the day, but seeing Ambrose Green do anything out of the ordinary was cause for comment.

Ambrose gave his customary grunt of agreement, and then added, "You ain't missing a kid, are you, Hornby?"

"A kid?" Jack Hornby asked. He climbed down from his boat and slowly approached Ambrose's. "The missus and I ain't been blessed yet, though we live in hope. Why?"

Ambrose jerked his chin towards the deck of his ship, and Jack Hornby drew close enough to see her.

"Well, would you look at that," he said. "No, she ain't mine. Prob'ly an orphan. Poor mite."

The little girl still hadn't moved.

"What's going on?" another voice shouted.

"Green's found a little kid in his boat," Hornby shouted back. "Wondering how she got there."

"That's new to me," the voice replied.

Ambrose bent down so that he was on the girl's eye level. "It's alright," he said softly to her. "No need to be scared."

The little girl smiled at him, revealing a gap between her two front teeth.

"Maybe the dock master'll know where she came from," Hornsby said, but he didn't sound very convinced. Ambrose nodded. He rose and turned to step out of the boat, and the little girl gave a cry of protest. She scurried across the deck toward him, stopping just out of reach. Ambrose stared at her, nonplussed.

"Looks like she likes you," Hornby said, laughing. Ambrose could not see how that could be true. But there was no denying that the girl had followed him, and was now looking up at him with large, pleading eyes.

"Come on," Ambrose said to her softly, holding out a hand. "Up you get."

The little girl put her tiny hand into his and pulled herself to her feet. She was as thin as a tree branch, with legs that looked too spindly to carry her weight and scrapes on both of her exposed knees. The rain continued to fall, and she shivered in the cold.

"Come on now," Ambrose said. "Let's go see where you belong." The little girl did not let go of his hand, so Ambrose found himself leading her carefully out of the boat and toward the dock master's offices.

The sun continued to rise as Ambrose spoke to the dock master, and to all the other fishermen he could find, but nobody had any idea who the little girl might be or how she had ended up in his boat. The promise of getting a good catch for the day was fading with every minute that Ambrose lingered on the shore, but what else was he supposed to do? The girl looked so helpless. He couldn't leave her here alone.

She looked hungry too, he decided. If she'd lost her parents, how long had it been since she'd eaten? He pulled the tarp back over his boat with the girl standing at his ankles, and then began to lead her away toward the market.

Old Jenny made no effort to hide her surprise at seeing him as he approached. "Mr Green!" she said. "As I live and breathe. Never thought I'd see you here so early in the morning. I hope there's nothing wrong with your boat."

Ambrose gave a grunt that could have been either agreement or disagreement. Old Jenny was never certain. "Found this little one hiding in there," he said gruffly, gesturing at the girl still standing close beside him. "Thought she looked hungry."

"Oh, you poor dear!" Old Jenny said, springing into action at once. "Sleeping in a fishing boat? Don't you know it isn't safe? Here." She spooned a generous helping of stew into a bowl, then went around the front of the stall and knelt down to hand it to the girl. The girl held the bowl with both hands and lifted it to her lips, slurping the stew down like it might disappear if she waited too long.

Ambrose tried to hand a penny over to Old Jenny, but she waved him away with a click of her tongue. "What are you going to do with her?" Old Jenny asked him.

Ambrose did not know. "See if someone recognises her," he said. "She must belong to someone."

"Well, I can ask around if anyone's missing a kid," Old Jenny said, but she sounded doubtful. "Could be she has no one, though. Too many kids without a soul to care for 'em these days. I see 'em too often in here, trying to sell a bit of junk for a bite to eat. Breaks my heart, it does."

"Could you watch her?" Ambrose asked. "While you ask around. I can't take her out on the boat."

Old Jenny looked a little reluctant, but she nodded anyway. "If she's anyone's," she said, "someone will recognise her around here eventually. Come on, dear," she added to the little girl. Placing a hand on her back, she steered her behind the stall. Ambrose nodded his thanks to her, the need for words now over, and began to turn away.

The little girl gave out a shriek of dismay, and a moment later, he felt a thud against his leg as she wrapped herself around it, clinging on as tightly as she could, the bowl of stew forgotten.

"Don't be silly, now," Ambrose said softly. "You know you can't stay with me."

The girl snuggled closer to his leg, shaking her head.

"I think she likes you," Old Jenny said with a smile.

Ambrose looked down at the girl. No one had expressed a modicum of affection for him since Peggy died. He could not imagine why this lonely little child would want to keep him close. But as the girl looked up at him with her wide green eyes, Ambrose felt an unfamiliar warmth in his heart.

"Alright, little one," he said softly. "Alright. You stick with me then. Just 'til we find out where you belong."

CHAPTER TWO

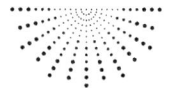

People at the market were surprisingly generous that day as Ambrose searched for food and warm clothes for the little girl. Mrs. Mason had a hand-knitted jumper that she claimed her daughter had grown too big for, and she handed it over free of charge, while Mr Smith at the cobbler's stall insisted that the tiny pair of boots that fit the girl were second hand, and so only cost ten pence, despite what Ambrose knew about the value of the leather alone. Ambrose assumed that the market stall holders were all as taken with the girl's wide eyes and bedraggled appearance as he was, and they felt compelled to help her, but although people were sympathetic towards the girl, Ambrose was the one who inspired the depth of their generosity. He had been a mainstay at the market for many years, and everyone knew the tragic story of his wife and unborn child. It was so surprising to see him breaking his routine and to hear him speak, to hear him emotionally invested in *anything*, that it warmed the heart of everyone who saw him to see him caring for the little girl, and although they all knew he would reject charity, when they considered his small fisherman's income, they all wanted to contribute what they could.

But nobody knew anything about the girl, where she had come from, or who her parents might be. She was distinctive enough, with her wild blonde hair and searching green eyes, but not a soul recognised her, not even as one of the orphan children who might scrabble around in the bins for scraps. It was as though she had appeared out of thin air, or, perhaps more fittingly, out of the sea itself, a little changeling girl with no past at all.

Ambrose knew that could not be true, but he also knew how harsh the world could be, and although he insisted he was going to find her family, he knew in the back of his mind that it was likely the girl had none. He took her back to his cottage that night and set her up with a warm pile of blankets, and she looked up at him with those same wide eyes and gap-toothed smile, saying nothing.

"You must have a name," Ambrose said. "You sure you don't want to share?"

The little girl said nothing.

"Well, I can't keep calling you 'girl'," Ambrose said. "How 'bout I call you Heather," he added. "Just for now, til we find out who you are. Would that suit you?" The girl's smile grew wider, showing more of her uneven teeth. "I'll take that as a yes," Ambrose said. "My wife always liked the name Heather," he added conversationally, as he moved to the stove to prepare a little supper for the girl. She was dreadfully thin. A little extra food wouldn't hurt her. "She was expecting a little one, and she said if it was a girl, she'd like to name it Heather. It's a plant, you know, out on the moors. Purple. Grows wild. My wife always said it meant freedom." The little girl watched him, taking in every word. "She died, though," he added, hardly knowing what he was saying. "Fifteen years back. Fifteen years today, in fact. The fever got her, and that little baby too. It's just been me ever since then. Just me." He nodded to himself, the words surprisingly comforting in the quiet of the evening. He was surprised to realise it, but he did not think he had ever spoken about his wife's death out loud to anyone. People around him had always just known, and he'd never felt the need to confide in them. Why would he? Words could not change what had happened. "Well, now," he said softly. "You've got me all reminiscing. How about that?"

When Ambrose awoke the next morning, he found Heather snuggled up beside him, still fast asleep with a gentle smile on her face. She woke up as he began his morning routine, preparing for the day, and skipped up to him as he made his coffee, looking curious. Ambrose handed her the mug, and she took a cautious sip, before twisting up her face in disgust.

Ambrose laughed. "Yeah, it's a little bitter," he said. "I make my own, but they have cocoa at the coffee stand near the docks. Might be more to your liking. What do you think? Want to grab some on the way?"

Heather considered him for a moment, and then nodded.

"So you do understand me," Ambrose said. "I was beginning to wonder. Come on, then."

The pair of them stopped at Mrs. Atha's coffee stand, and Ambrose handed over a couple of coins in exchange for hot drinks for them both. Heather cradled the hot cocoa in her hands, taking careful sips, while Ambrose gulped down his second coffee of the morning. He did not know what Mrs. Atha put in it that was different from the beans and hot water he made at home, but he had to admit that it was delicious.

A fishing boat did not seem like a safe place for a little girl, but when Ambrose attempted to leave her in the care of the dock master's wife for the day, she screamed and screamed until Ambrose relented. Heather sat in the corner of the fishing boat with a tarp wrapped around her to protect her from the cold of the water, and her wide eyes followed Ambrose as he went about his work. She did not move or make a sound, her expression as calm as the deep blue sea when not a single breath of wind disturbed it. Ambrose found himself talking to her as he worked, showing her the different types of knots and talking her through the process of setting up the nets.

Heather listened attentively, and Ambrose found that he liked the rhythm of it. He had been alone for many years now, and he had never wanted a companion in all that time, but Heather was different, somehow. It felt as though she had always been there, and he already knew he would miss her when she had to leave.

They sold their catch at the market that afternoon, but no one had any news about what Heather's origins might be, and Heather still wasn't speaking. So Ambrose took her out with him to sea the next day, and the next, until people stopped wondering at the origins of the little girl at his side, and just started to think of her as his.

Ambrose never gave much thought to God or religion. Although it comforted him to think of his wife in Heaven, waiting for him to join her, it hurt him deeply to remember that he had lost her too soon, and he always thought that perhaps God was too busy to concern Himself with a man like him. But now he looked at Heather, and he thought surely the Lord must have brought her to him. On a day of great heartache and loss, he had found hope and purpose again.

So when Heather finally spoke, a few weeks after he found her in the boat, to call him "Papa," Ambrose could not stop a few tears from forming in his eyes. Heather was his life now, he thought, his purpose and his future, and he would do anything for her to be happy.

CHAPTER THREE

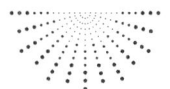

Heather remained something of a spindly girl, but she flourished under Ambrose's care. She still spoke little, but when she did, her voice was clear as a bell. Ambrose was rarely ever seen without her. It didn't take long for them to settle into a new routine. With a little help from Old Jenny and Ambrose's knot-tying experience, he learned to braid her blonde hair so that it did not get in the way when they were out on the sea, and every morning after washing her face, Heather would sit on a little stool in their home and he would sort her hair for the day.

Ambrose still made his own coffee at home, unable to bear the thought of heading out into the cold and dark of the morning without it, but after that first morning, he and Heather always stopped by Mrs. Atha's on the way to the docks and bought a second, sweeter coffee for Ambrose and a hot cocoa for the girl.

Heather took to the sea like she had been born to it, and sometimes Ambrose thought perhaps she had, considering how he had first found her. Her little fingers were far defter than Ambrose's had ever been, and the pair of them worked in tandem with the need for barely a word between them. Heather was still far too young to haul the nets, but she lightened the load in other ways, and Ambrose always felt at peace as long as she was working alongside him.

At the end of the day, they would go to the market to sell their catch, and then get a stew from Old Jenny to warm their bones. Old Jenny adored Heather, and constantly snuck her extra treats, a luxury that Ambrose pretended to feel stern about, but secretly enjoyed very much.

But by the time Heather turned six, Ambrose began to worry that life in a fishing boat was not what his daughter needed most. He loved her, and he had taught her a trade, he supposed, but other children around her age were going to school and learning to read and write. Ambrose had never learned himself, but if little Heather were to have the best chance in life, she would need to learn. And she was smart, he thought, smart enough to learn that and more besides.

So one day, after they had purchased their hot drinks and were making their way towards the docks, Ambrose cleared his throat and spoke. "Heather," he said, his voice a little raspy. She looked up at him over the top of her cocoa and smiled. "You're getting older now. I think maybe it's time for a change."

She frowned, the smile falling from her face. "What do you mean, Papa?" she asked.

"I mean," he said, "that I think you need to start going to school. Learn some things that aren't fishing and the sea."

She shook her head at once. "I don't want to, Papa," she said. "I want to stay with you."

"You will be staying with me," he said. "Don't worry your head about that. But you can't spend every day on the boat. You need an education."

"You can teach me," Heather said, with all the conviction of a child who still believed her father knew everything about the world. "Teach me on the boat."

"I can't," Ambrose said. "I don't know enough. I was never good at school. I want you to learn *more* than me, alright?"

"I can't go to school," Heather said pragmatically. "Who will help you on the boat?"

"I'll make do, Heather," Ambrose said.

But Heather shook her head. "I'll miss you," she said. "I won't go."

"How about a compromise?" Ambrose said. "So we can both be happy. You go to school four days a week, and come out on the boat with me the other three. Then you can tell me all about what you're learning while we're working, eh?"

Heather was still reluctant, but Ambrose was firm. He wanted everything for his daughter, and school was essential for her to have any sort of future. Heather turned out to be a bit of a loner at the church school, like Ambrose himself, rarely talking to the other children and just sitting with her own thoughts while the others ran around and played, but she took quickly to her letters and her figures. In the months that followed, it delighted Ambrose to see Heather attempting to read out any signs that they passed, and their days on the boat were filled with chatter about kings and queens and faraway places and Heather practicing her counting and her letters.

As the years passed, Heather became quite an admirable little scholar in Ambrose's eyes. She was quick and smart, and he could tell that she longed for more learning than the little free church school and Ambrose's meagre fishing income could provide. She often went to the newsagents, looking for something new to read, and bought as many penny novels as she could, but Ambrose saw the covers and he worried that these tales of monsters and brigands weren't exactly the sort of reading material to cultivate a young lady's mind.

When Heather grew too old for the church school, Ambrose began to send her to the watchful eye of his neighbour's wife, Mrs. Alcott, where she learned about sewing and housekeeping and taking care of children.

Heather found these sessions even more tedious than she had ever found school, but Ambrose insisted that a girl needed to learn these things.

"But I don't want to get married and have children," Heather said stubbornly one day on the boat. "I want to stay with you."

"I won't be around forever," he said. "I need to know you'll be taken care of when I'm gone."

Heather sniffed. "I can take care of myself, Papa," she said. "I don't need a husband to do that."

But Ambrose had spent fifteen years of his life alone, mourning his wife Peggy, and he knew that being able to take care of oneself was not always enough. He did not want Heather to simply survive. He wanted her to flourish and be cherished, as she deserved. He did not like to think of her alone once he was forced to depart this world.

Yet Ambrose knew that the meagre education available to her was not near what Heather deserved. It was somewhat radical, he knew, to think of educating a girl beyond the basics, but Heather devoured new ideas with such passion that it seemed a crime to deny her. He could not afford a tutor for her, or even to buy fancy books that might teach her more than those sensationalised novels, but he wished he could give her more.

When Heather was thirteen, a letter arrived for Ambrose in the post. This was an extremely rare occurrence, although Heather had taught him a little more of letters than he had retained from school, he and the people of his acquaintance still wrote and read very little. He handed the letter over to Heather, and she read it silently with a slight frown on her face for a moment before announcing its contents out loud.

"It's from a woman called Aunt Ida," she said. "From Wakefield."

"Ah, she was your mother's aunt," Ambrose said. He had long ago forgotten that Heather was not truly his daughter in blood, and spoke about his late wife Peggy as if Heather was their child.

"Where's Wakefield?" Heather asked.

"About a hundred miles away," Ambrose said. "The next county over, in Yorkshire. But the other side of Yorkshire, I think. I've never been myself."

"She says she's coming back to Grimsby to take in the sea air," Heather said. "That's good, isn't it? It must be sad for the people who live in the middle of the country, without any chance to see the water. She says she'll be here next week. Did she used to live here, then?"

Ambrose nodded. "She helped your grandmother raise your mother, when your mother was very small. Then she married a far richer man than me, a factory owner, and moved away. Your mother told me she missed her a lot when she first left, and she used to write to her aunt a lot.

She was good with her words, not like me. You take after her with that."

"Aunt Ida wants to see us," Heather said, scanning the letter again. "If we can spare the time. Oh, can we meet her, Papa? She must be a very fancy lady, to be able to travel all this way. And we could take her out in the boat!"

"I don't think she'd like that so much," Ambrose said with a smile, "but we can definitely meet her on dry land. Write back for me, won't you, Heather?" Heather smiled and nodded. Ambrose said no more, but his mind was working fast. Aunt Ida was what anyone around here would call rich, and Peggy had always had the fondest memories of her. Perhaps she could do something for Heather and her education. A girl needed opportunities and connections and friends, and a woman like Aunt Ida might be able to provide them.

He did not mention these thoughts to Heather. His daughter would cry, he knew, if she thought he was even considering sending her away, and might refuse to meet Aunt Ida at all in response. She was stubborn like that. Stubborn like her father. But perhaps if Heather and Aunt Ida met and liked each other, he thought, Heather would see it as an opportunity and become excited to go.

It was all theoretical, of course. Aunt Ida might not even be able to help Heather, but if it worked out, Ambrose thought, he might finally be able to give Heather the future that she deserved.

CHAPTER FOUR

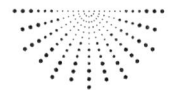

When Aunt Ida arrived, Heather's suspicions were confirmed that she was a very fancy woman indeed. She looked utterly out of place beside the pair of them as they took a walk through the park. Her waist was cinched in tight with a corset, and her skirts were so wide and heavy that she took up twice as much space on the pavement as Heather and Ambrose combined. Her grey hair was pulled back into an elegant knot, with a feathered hat balanced atop it. She carried a parasol to protect her skin from the summer sun, and she spoke little. With Ambrose also reluctant to speak around anyone other than his daughter, it fell to Heather to maintain the conversation, and she alternated between telling Aunt Ida all about her school and their adventures on the sea, and asking her about Wakefield and Yorkshire and the life she had led. Heather also asked Aunt Ida about Peggy, calling her Mamma, and Aunt Ida obliged with tales of the happy baby and meddlesome toddler she had known before she married and moved out of Grimsby.

Heather was oblivious to Aunt Ida's assessing glances, but Ambrose noticed them, and he felt ashamed. Aunt Ida was clearly disapproving of Heather's dress and manner, and it was only compared to the finest of Aunt Ida's comportment that Ambrose saw how unusually outspoken and rough accented his daughter was. Her hair was frizzy from the salt in the air around the sea, and her tanned skin was covered in freckles. She wore a simple grey dress with very little shape, and her hair was in the same braid that it always was, and Ambrose could tell that Aunt Ida approved of neither. He knew that Heather was an intelligent, kind-hearted, spirited girl, and it caused him great pain to see how a woman of society responded to her. If she had had a mother, Ambrose thought, and if he had not taken her out fishing with him, she would have been better off. All he could do now is try to make amends.

"An interesting girl," Aunt Ida said softly, after Ambrose sent Heather off to the market so that he could speak to the woman alone.

"She's very bright," Ambrose said. "But I worry about her, stuck with only me for company. She's too clever for me."

"It must have been hard for her," Aunt Ida said, "growing up without a mother."

"I did what I could," Ambrose said.

"Of course," Aunt Ida said. "But she needs a female hand, to guide her in matters of womanhood. No man, no matter how well-intentioned, can teach her that." Aunt Ida was quiet for a few moments. "I should like to take her back to Wakefield with me," she said.

"Take her back to Wakefield?" Ambrose said. It was what he had secretly hoped for, but as soon as Aunt Ida said it aloud, he wished he could take the thought back. He did not want to be without his Heather.

"She is bright," Aunt Ida said, "but rough and unmannered. If she were to come with me, I could teach her a little more deportment."

Ambrose reminded himself of all the advantages of such an offer, even as his heart screamed at him to refuse. "I know she wants to learn more of the world."

"There is a girls' school in town," Aunt Ida said, "that I think would suit her nicely. And if you would not be opposed, she could help a little with the running of my late husband's factory. Nothing too strenuous, of course, but it would give her skills that would benefit her greatly, I believe."

"Your husband's factory?" Ambrose asked, feeling unsure.

"Well, my factory now," she said. "Along with my son, Matthew. She would learn a great deal."

"I could not afford much for her upkeep," Ambrose said.

"Nonsense," Aunt Ida said. "She is my great-niece, and I remember her mother fondly. She is more than welcome to return with me."

"That is very kind of you," Ambrose said. "I'm sure she will be delighted."

∽

Heather, predictably, was not delighted by the news. "Papa, I *can't* go to Wakefield," she said. "I need to stay with you."

"I'll be alright, Heather," he said gruffly. "You're the one I'm worried about. There's a whole world out there. Don't you want to see it?"

"Not if I have to leave you," Heather said. She had tears in her eyes, and the sight was enough to break Ambrose's heart. "I'm happy here, Papa."

"I know you are, darling," Ambrose said. "But there are things you need that I can't offer you. You can't spend your whole life going out in the boat with me. There are things you need to learn that I can't teach you."

"Then I don't want to learn them," Heather said. "Papa, I'll be miserable without you."

"You won't be," Ambrose said. "You'll have so much to do, and so many exciting new people to meet, that you'll soon forget all about your old papa."

"That is not true," Heather said. "That could never be true."

"I hope it can be true," Ambrose said. "You deserve more than this."

Heather shook her head, her tears spilling down her cheeks.

"It's not forever," Ambrose said, although it caused him great pain to say it. "We will still see each other. And if you want to move back to Grimsby once your education is complete, you can." Secretly, Ambrose thought that was unlikely to happen, but he could not tell the crying child that her heart would change in time. It would only upset her more to imagine there would be a time when she would not feel like this. "It'll be a real school, Heather. A real one. Think how much you'll have to read, outside those penny novels. Real books. And your Aunt Ida adores you. She will teach you so many things."

Heather sniffed. "And you'll visit?"

"If you want me to," Ambrose said. He took his daughter's hands in his and squeezed them firmly. "It's for the best, Heather. You'll see."

A few days later, Heather stood on the platform at Grimsby train station with Aunt Ida and her father beside her. She eyed the large metal contraption suspiciously as

Aunt Ida fussed with a porter over the movement of her luggage. Heather's own bag was still in her hands. She had few enough possessions, and the clothes she did have would hardly be suitable at her destination.

"Now you be good," her father said, putting a firm hand on her shoulder. "Do you hear?"

"I will," Heather said. "I promise."

"You learn to be a fine young lady. Make your mother proud."

"I hope I'll make you proud too, Papa," Heather said.

"I'm proud of you every day, Heather," he said. "Don't you worry about that."

"Well, that's all sorted," Aunt Ida said, striding over to the pair before Heather could reply. "Come along, Heather. The train will be departing soon."

Heather nodded. She had tears in her eyes, but she tried to blink them away. She did not want her papa to think of her crying when he looked back on this moment. Instead, she threw her arms around him, pulling him into a hug. Slowly, he hugged her back.

"I love you, Papa," she said softly.

Her father could not put his own feelings into words, but Heather saw the tears in his own eyes, and she understood.

CHAPTER FIVE

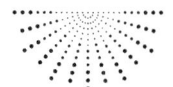

The countryside flew past the window as the train chugged its way inland. The view outside was half concealed by the thick smoke billowing from the engine, and passengers had to speak loudly to be heard over the rattle of the wheels beneath them.

Heather and Aunt Ida sat alone in a compartment. As soon as the train had departed, Aunt Ida had pulled a little embroidery out of her bag, and she was working on it as though the shake and noise of the train were utterly unremarkable. Heather, for her part, continued to look out of the window at the unfamiliar hills and fields. Her beloved sea had already vanished from view, and her father was lost along with it. She could not cry more in front of Aunt Ida, not when she was being so generous and offering Heather such an opportunity, so she tried to focus on the swaying landscape, squeezing her hands in her lap.

"You must work very hard," Aunt Ida said to her, after about half an hour had passed. "I have no room for wastrels in my home."

"I will," Heather said, a little startled. Aunt Ida sounded much sterner than she had when she had spoken previously.

"Make certain that you do," Aunt Ida said. "You're a smart girl."

"Thank you, Aunt Ida."

"The correct response is to deny it," Aunt Ida said, pursing her lips in disapproval. "Humility is a great virtue for a young woman. Vanity most certainly is not."

"I'm sorry, Aunt Ida," Heather said. Her father had told her that she must defer to Aunt Ida in all things, so although her words felt cruel, Heather forced herself to look and feel contrite. "I did not mean it that way."

"You must mind your words and actions are not misinterpreted," Aunt Ida said. "It takes very little to ruin even a virtuous girl's reputation, and you are certainly not that."

"Aunt Ida?" Heather asked.

"It is not your fault, of course, growing up as you have," Aunt Ida said. "But it will take a lot of work to repair the ill that your fisherwoman life has done to you." She said *fisherwoman* as though it were an insult.

"Papa said I was to go to school again," Heather said.

"Eventually," Aunt Ida said, looking back at her embroidery. "When you are ready. We will have to work on your rough edges first. They will never accept you as you are."

"I'm sorry, Aunt Ida," Heather said softly.

"It's not your fault, dear," Aunt Ida said. "I will do what I can."

They were forced to transfer trains after a while, and the journey took about three hours in all. Heather never quite adjusted to the sway of the carriage. Aunt Ida spoke little after their initial conversation, and Heather was left to sit in silence with her thoughts. Her head ached, but she decided to blame it on the train, and not on Aunt Ida's words. She had been under the impression that Aunt Ida had liked her, but from her words on the journey, she thought Heather an uncouth girl. It stung Heather's heart to think that she had already disappointed her guardian and failed in her promise to her father to make him proud. She vowed that she would listen to Aunt Ida's instructions and make amends.

They alighted from the train at Wakefield station and waited for the porter to appear with Aunt Ida's bags. Aunt Ida acquired a cab in front of the station, and soon she and Heather were making their way through the city streets, towards Heather's new home.

"We live close to the factory," Aunt Ida said to Heather as the cab rattled along. "It makes things easier that way. You will be going there for your shifts, of course. But I will leave it to my son to explain the details."

"Is he my father's age?" Heather asked.

"He is twenty five," Aunt Ida said. She narrowed her eyes at Heather. "But do not be getting ideas in your head. He is married, and no match for you either way."

Heather did not understand what ideas Aunt Ida could possibly mean, but Aunt Ida seemed furious about the possibility of Heather developing them, so she looked at her lap and said, "I won't, Aunt Ida."

The cab pulled up outside a large brick house, and Aunt Ida and Heather climbed out. As Aunt Ida paid the driver, Heather looked about. Across the road, behind high stone walls and a fearsome looking metal gate, was a huge building that could only be the factory. She could hear the whirr of the machines, even from this distance. It looked like a stern and depressing sort of place, and Heather shivered despite herself. A river bent around behind it, its churning dark water so different from the sea that she knew.

"Stop gawking, Heather, and come along," Aunt Ida said.

Heather tore her eyes away from the factory and followed Aunt Ida into the house.

The front hall was narrow and dark, with deep red wallpaper covering the walls. A faint layer of dust clung to the sideboards, and the windows were lined with grime. "The last maid quit just before I left for Grimsby," Aunt Ida said. "I see my daughter-in-law has taken no steps to replace her."

Aunt Ida led the way into the sitting room. Heather looked about, taking in every detail, from the dusty wooden floors to the fine silver candlesticks on the mantelpiece. A woman sat on a long sofa, sipping tea. "Mother," she said, when Aunt Ida entered the room. "I did not know we would be seeing you today."

"I cannot be gone long, Edna," Aunt Ida said. "I know my son."

The woman named Edna took a good look at Heather, and she raised her eyebrows. She was an elegant looking woman in her twenties, narrow faced and fashionably dressed, and Heather sensed instantly that she disapproved of Heather's appearance.

"This is the girl you wrote about?" Edna said.

"Yes," Aunt Ida replied. "Heather is our new ward."

"Hm," Edna replied noncommittally. "Perhaps she will come in useful."

Heather did not know how to reply, so she bobbed into a curtsey, and Edna sneered. "What a funny little thing," she said. "Wherever did you find her?"

"The fishing docks," Aunt Ida said, and Edna laughed, although Heather could not have said why. "She will polish up well enough."

"If you say so, Mother," Edna said.

Aunt Ida led Heather up the stairs, and then up another, narrower flight, until they reached the wooden walls and floor of the attic. Aunt Ida pushed open a door at the end of the corridor, revealing a small room with a single bed, a chest for clothes, and a water basin. A small window allowed in a little light, but the overall effect was grim compared to the loving cosiness of her father's cottage by the sea.

"This will be your room," Aunt Ida said. "Dinner is at seven. We manage to keep a cook, at least, but I know you will want to rest after your journey. I will have her bring up some bread and stew for you, so you can eat it here."

"Alright," Heather said uncertainly. She did feel tired and more than a little overwhelmed. Aunt Ida nodded at her and pulled the door closed behind her, and Heather sank onto the bed. The mattress was as solid as stone, but Heather pulled her legs onto it and curled up on top of the blankets, her cheek pressed against the pillow. Now that no one else was around to see her, she allowed her tears to fall.

She missed her papa and her home and the smell of the nearby sea. Everything here was grim and dark, and she did not know how to live in a fancy house like this, or get along with a new family, or meet Aunt Ida's expectations. For the first time she could remember, she felt deeply lonely, and she wrapped her arms around herself, holding herself tight as her tears slid onto the pillow. She was doing this for her papa, she told herself. She was going to make him proud. But at that moment, all she really wanted was to hear his soothing voice and see his loving face before her again.

CHAPTER SIX

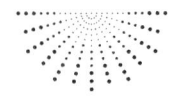

Heather awoke with the sun the following morning, as had been her habit for as long as she could remember. The room that Aunt Ida had given her contained no new clothes, so she dressed in another of her loose grey dresses and braided her hair quickly behind her head. She only hoped Aunt Ida would not be angry with her for her provincial appearance.

A bowl of cold stew and some bread had been placed just inside the door. Heather had been so exhausted that she must have slept through the cook's arrival. Heather's stomach growled, so she ate it now, even though it was cold, licking her fingers once she was done. She had just picked up the bowl and moved to open the door when she heard sharp footsteps out in the corridor.

Aunt Ida was marching towards her, looking stern. "Good," she said, when she saw Heather in the doorway.

"You're up. Your job is to clean the house today. It has truly got into an atrocious state. Start with the entrance hall downstairs. Cook can provide you with a mop and bucket. At noon, I need you to go to the factory. My son Matthew will meet you and inform you what is to be done there. You can eat once you return."

Heather was suddenly very glad she had eaten the cold stew before Aunt Ida had appeared. "Do you only normally eat in the evening here?"

"*You* will eat in the evenings," Aunt Ida said, "once your work is done. It will provide you with some extra motivation. Goodness knows you will probably need it."

Heather wanted to argue, but she remembered what she had promised her father, and she bit her tongue. "Yes, Aunt Ida," she said instead. Aunt Ida just wanted the best for her, she told herself. She was working to rid her of the rough edges. It would be difficult, but it would be worth it when Heather saw her father smile again.

Heather worked hard all morning, dusting and mopping the entrance hall and then moving to clean the sitting room. It was slow, tiring work, but Heather was strong after a childhood in the fishing boat with her father, and she thought she worked efficiently enough. While in the sitting room, she paused to consider one of the bookshelves, reading the many titles on the spines there. These were no penny novels from the newsagents. Each volume was bound in elegant leather, with gleaming gilt letters and ribbons attached to the spine. Heather ran her fingertips along them, and they came back coated with dust. These books were not loved, she thought, as she applied her dusting cloth to them. But she would love them, once her work was done.

But the house was a large and filthy place, and Heather had not even cleaned a quarter of it before Aunt Ida shouted at her and ferried her across the road to the factory. Aunt Ida did not have a word of praise for Heather's efforts, but simply sniffed that she had thought she would have made more progress, and that being a fisherman's daughter apparently was no guarantee against laziness. Heather felt the sting of the words, after spending the entire morning toiling away alone, but she reminded herself again of Aunt Ida's promise to her father, and accepted that there must be some flaw in work that she was as yet too ignorant to see.

As Heather walked through the iron gates of the factory, the noise of the machines inside grew louder, and Heather fought the urge to flinch. She had never walked into either a prison or a workhouse, but she imagined this is what it felt like, a sinking feeling in your chest as you passed through stern gates that would not allow you to leave freely again. Heather's heart hammered as Aunt Ida led her to the factory entrance, and everything inside her screamed at her not to go inside. It was the exact opposite of everything she knew and loved. Instead of the open sky over the sea, there were plain stone walls and a severe looking roof. Instead of the fresh salt on the air, she smelt smoke and sweat.

The air inside the factory was thick with a white substance that Heather could not name. It clung to the air that she breathed, drawn into her lungs, and she coughed.

"Cotton," Aunt Ida said. "It gets everywhere."

She led Heather to an office where a tall brown-haired man sat working behind a desk. He had Aunt Ida's strong nose, and he stood respectfully when she entered the room.

"Mother," he said. "This is the girl, I take it." He gave Heather an assessing look, his gaze sliding from head to toe and back up again, lingering here and there as he went. "She doesn't look like much," he said, turning away with a slight sneer.

"She's not," Aunt Ida said, "but she will be useful. Her father wishes her to learn about the textile industry."

"Does he now?" Matthew said, with little interest. "And we are to teach her?"

"I will put her on the machines," Aunt Ida said. "An eight hour shift. That should give her education enough for now."

"I assume we're not expected to pay her," Matthew said.

"She's paid with room and board," Aunt Ida said, "and our

generosity. I will leave her to you." And without another word to Heather, she swept from the room.

Matthew turned his back to Heather and began searching through the papers on his desk. Heather stood looking at him, waiting for further instructions, but they did not come.

"Sir?" she said, after a few minutes.

"Yes, yes," he said distractedly. "Heather, is it?"

"Yes, sir," she said.

"Have you ever worked in a factory or a mill before, Heather?"

"No, sir," Heather said. "Never."

He sighed in disapproval. "Follow me, then. Let's get this over with."

As soon as they left his office, Heather could taste the cotton in the air again. It was suffocating. Heather struggled not to cough as Matthew led her into a long room full of deafeningly loud machines. It was so hot in there that Heather felt she might faint. Many women and even girls younger than Heather worked the machines, while a man stood on a balcony at the far end, watching them.

"This one," Matthew shouted over the noise, gesturing to an empty post with his head. "Watch and learn. And be careful of your fingers. You're no use to anyone if you lose them."

Heather turned to ask for further instructions, but he was already striding away. A nearby woman glanced at her, but no one approached her or made any effort to speak to her. They were too absorbed in the rigour of their own work.

Eventually, watching the women around her, Heather was able to figure out what she was supposed to do. But the machines were terrifyingly loud, and hers moved so quickly and relentlessly that Heather feared it might rip off her whole arm if she made a mistake.

By the end of her eight hour shift, Heather was exhausted, both mentally and physically. Her head pounded from the noise of the machines, and her lungs felt wooly, as though the cotton of the air had settled inside. Her dress was stuck to her back with sweat, and tears stung her eyes as she made her wobbly way back toward the house.

Even outside the factory was no relief. She could still hear the machines across the street, and smoke billowed from the factory chimney, covering everything in soot and grime. Heather wiped her face with an equally dirty hand and stumbled toward the front door.

Before she reached it, Edna threw it open. "No," she said, after one glance at Heather. "You're filthy! Come in the back door."

"The back door?" Heather asked. She was too exhausted to think.

"Yes, the back door! Around the back! Go on!" Edna snapped, and Heather had enough wherewithal to obey. She stumbled around the back of the house, where she found a door that led into the kitchen. A woman in her fifties was cleaning the stove when Heather entered, and she frowned at Heather too.

"Don't be getting that grime in my kitchen," she said. "I won't have it. Here." She shoved a half-full bowl of stew toward Heather. "Your supper."

Heather looked at the meagre portion and grimaced. "Could I have a little more?" she asked. "I haven't eaten all day."

"The mistress said you were to get a half portion tonight," the cook said, "since you only did less than half of the work she expected from you."

"I worked non-stop all day," Heather protested.

"Whether you did or you didn't is nothing to me," the cook said, "and it's nothing to your aunt, either, I'd reckon. When she asks for a job done, she expects it done, and that's the end of it."

Heather nodded. She could not think what else to say. With a slight curtsey, she left the kitchen with her small bowl of stew and headed up to her attic room. She was so exhausted that it took great effort to make herself wash herself down and change into a nightdress before collapsing on the bed.

She had thought, coming here, that she would go to school and that Aunt Ida would teach her home management and details about the textiles trade. But it was only the first day, she told herself, even as tears ran down her cheeks. It would take time to adjust. Perhaps this was how all aunts acted when their uncouth nieces first came for lessons in deportment.

Heather was not a fool. She knew how unlikely that idea was, but all she could do was hope, so she wrapped the blanket tightly around her, and cried herself to sleep.

CHAPTER SEVEN

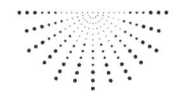

Months passed, and nothing changed beyond the weather. Aunt Ida rarely spoke to Heather except to berate her, and Matthew ignored her entirely. She worked sixteen hours a day, first cleaning the house as hard as she could and then working a shift at the factory, and if her work was considered unsatisfactory, her portion at dinner was cut as a result.

Heather soon realised she was to be the sole person responsible for cleaning. Aunt Ida spoke of a maid who had lived in the house previously, but she made no move to hire another one to replace her, and Matthew's wife Edna never lifted a finger of her own to help. There was less work to do once Heather had finished her initial thorough clean of the house, but the smoke from the factory covered everything with a layer of grime almost as soon as Heather had finished cleaning it, and the rest of the family members were careless and lazy, leaving objects strewn about and expecting Heather to return them to their proper place. Heather's least favourite day was Monday, laundry day, when she spent her entire morning washing clothes and running them through a mangle, and the entire afternoon and evening at the machine in the factory. It was an entire day of intense physical labour, and as she had very little time to get through all the laundry she was assigned, these were the days when she most often ended up going hungry. Her favourite day was Sunday, because on Sundays the factory was closed. Heather still had to do extra chores at home with her free afternoon, but at least she was not surrounded by the deafening rattle of the machinery, and the air around her was not thick with cotton.

Heather worked up the courage to ask Aunt Ida about her education several times, but Aunt Ida always dismissed her, saying she had yet to earn her place. Heather forced herself to have hope for many months, because what else could she do? Eventually, she was forced to accept that Aunt Ida was not cruel to her for her own good, but simply because Aunt Ida was cruel, and that she had no intention of ever giving Heather the education she was promised. Heather was simply free labour at home and at the factory, and Aunt Ida would never give that up so that Heather could attend school.

She considered writing a letter to her papa, but he couldn't read. Even if he got someone else to help him, Heather had no material to write on and no money to pay for postage. Aunt Ida would be furious if she thought Heather had stolen from her, and Heather did not like to imagine what the punishment would be for that.

Finally, Heather steeled her courage together and went to visit Aunt Ida in her study. Aunt Ida frowned when Heather knocked on the open door. "Yes?" she said. "What is it, Heather?"

"Aunt Ida," Heather said. "I really appreciate everything you have done for me. But I was hoping I could write to my papa. I miss him terribly. I was hoping to go back to Grimsby and visit him." Lying was a sin, Heather knew, but if she could only see her papa in person, she could tell him the truth of what had been happening, and he would know what to do.

Aunt Ida just rolled her eyes. "You have no money for the train," she said.

"Perhaps Papa could send some," Heather said. "If we wrote to him."

Aunt Ida considered her for a long moment, and Heather felt certain she was going to refuse her. Then she nodded. "Very well," she said. "I will write to your father, and if he can spare money for the train for you, you may visit for a few days."

"Thank you, Aunt Ida," Heather said, bobbing into a curtsey.

"Yes, yes," Aunt Ida said. "Now leave me, please. I have developed quite a headache."

⁓

All Heather's work felt easier in the week that followed her conversation with her aunt. Even the oppressiveness of the factory was more bearable when she thought of seeing her father's face again. Perhaps they might even go out on the sea, she thought, and life would be like it was before Aunt Ida came into it, at least for a little while. Once she told her Papa the truth of how Aunt Ida treated her in Wakefield, she was certain he would keep her in Grimsby with him. He would not blame Heather for the failure of the scheme, she knew. He would be furious with Aunt Ida for her mistreatment of his daughter, and everything would go back to how it had been before.

When Aunt Ida approached Heather one morning as she dusted the shelves in the study, Heather stood up straight immediately, a smile spreading across her face despite herself. The money had come.

But Aunt Ida had a grave expression on her face, and Heather hesitated, suddenly afraid.

"I have bad news, Heather," Aunt Ida said.

Heather put a hand on the shelves beside her to steady herself. "What is it?" she asked.

"I received word from Grimsby," Aunt Ida said. "I am afraid your father has died."

"No," Heather said. The words did not make sense. "That can't be true."

"It is true," Aunt Ida said. "He had a fishing accident. He died at sea."

Heather shook her head. The world around her had turned very loud and very still. "If it was at sea, how do they know?" she asked.

"His boat floated back to shore," Aunt Ida said. "Wrecked, without him in it."

"But Papa is a good sailor," Heather said. "He's done it for years. He would never take any risks."

"Perhaps," Aunt Ida said, "he pushed himself to try and earn extra money to pay for your visit." Aunt Ida spoke mildly, but Heather recoiled as though she had been slapped. Could it be true? Her Papa, dead, because of her request?

"No," she said again.

"Yes," Aunt Ida said firmly. "Denying it will not make it less true."

Heather stared at a spot on the wall behind Aunt Ida's head. Her legs swayed beneath her, and she gripped the shelf harder to keep herself upright.

"You may remain here, of course," Aunt Ida said, "as long as you conduct yourself properly. I took on responsibility for your care, and I intend to see it through. So you need not worry on that account."

"Thank you," Heather said softly. She hardly knew what she was saying. "When did it happen?" she asked suddenly.

"I have just received the letter," Aunt Ida said. "The accident was a few days past."

Heather's knees gave out. The world tilted around her, and she crashed to the floor. Aunt Ida was saying something else to her, her voice harsh, but Heather could not hear her any more. She stared at the floor as it blurred before her, the news echoing dully through her head. Her father was dead. *Dead.*

In that moment, she felt as though she had joined him. She felt hollowed out, like the world around her was no longer real at all. Aunt Ida was shouting at her now, but she could not make out the words, as though Aunt Ida were speaking to her through water. *This is what drowning feels like*, she thought, as she stared and stared. Aunt Ida grabbed her arm and shook her, but Heather did not even look at her.

Her papa was dead. Nothing else mattered now.

CHAPTER EIGHT

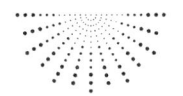

Heather lay in her bed for several days, hardly sleeping and refusing to eat. Aunt Ida shouted at her about her missed work, calling her a lazy, foolish girl, threatening to rethink her offer of a home if she did not move and pull her own weight, but Heather ignored it all. What did it matter, what Aunt Ida thought of her now? What did it matter if she ended up on the street? Her papa was dead, and she was alone in the world.

Finally, in desperation, Aunt Ida summoned a doctor for her great niece. At twenty two, Dr. David Armstrong was young for a man of his profession, and so somewhat more affordable than the other men Aunt Ida might have chosen from, but despite his youth, he was an excellent doctor, with a quick mind and a gentle heart. He knew what the problem was as soon as Aunt Ida spoke to him, but he went up to see Heather anyway, feeling her pulse and listening to the beat of her heart.

"Heartbreak," he told Aunt Ida, "and grief. She is very young to have lost so much so suddenly. She will come out of it in time."

"But she refuses to eat," Aunt Ida said. "I do not know when she last had water. She is killing herself, Dr. Armstrong."

"Not deliberately," Dr. Armstrong said. "She has just lost the will to go on. We must give her a reason to." He leaned over and took Heather's hand. "Miss Green," he said. "Miss Green, you can hear me, can't you?"

Heather looked at him. It was the only sign she was listening, but it was enough. "Miss Green, your father would not want you to perish for grief of him. He would want you to live on and be happy. He would want you to be here to remember him." Heather continued to look in his eyes, a slight frown forming on her face.

"He would want you to eat, Miss Green," he said. "You will waste away otherwise."

"I don't feel hungry," Heather murmured. They were the first words she had spoken in days, and they came out rough and raspy.

"But you still must eat," Dr. Armstrong said. "Please try. Here." He helped her into a sitting position and then turned back to Aunt Ida. "Perhaps you could fetch her a little broth," he said. "Something light."

Heather managed to swallow a few spoonsful of the broth, and a little while later, she ate a few more. It gave her a little strength, not enough to ease the pain in her heart, but enough for her to recognise the truth of Dr. Armstrong's words. Papa would not wish her to suffer in his absence. She had to make of life what she could.

Still, Dr. Armstrong prescribed a few more days' rest, followed by a regime of fresh air and walks, and he visited repeatedly over the following week. Aunt Ida scoffed at the idea of walks being necessary. If Heather could walk, she muttered to herself, she could work, but Heather's collapse seemed to have frightened her enough that she did not contradict the doctor's advice. Heather found herself walking along the river bank, looking at the churning water and remembering times on the sea with her father. It took surprisingly little time to escape the noise of the looms of the factories and mills along the riverside and find herself back in nature again. It was a very different sort of nature than she was accustomed to in Grimsby, with ferns and brambles and rolling hills, but Heather thought that her father would have enjoyed it.

On another walk, she ventured farther into town, towards the cathedral at its heart. She wove through market stalls assembled on the paving outside the grand building, debating whether to enter the cathedral itself or just wander through the graveyard and perhaps sit on the steps outside to take in the air.

"Miss Green," a voice called, and she turned, startled. She had no acquaintances in Wakefield other than her family.

Dr. Armstrong was walking towards her, smiling. He tipped his hat to her. "Good day to you, Miss Green," Dr. Armstrong said. "It is good to see you out and about again."

"Thank you, doctor," Heather said. "And thank you for helping me, before. I was lost."

"It is always difficult," Dr. Armstrong said, "to lose a parent. My father passed away a few months back too, and the pain is difficult to bear at times."

"I'm sorry for your loss," Heather said.

He nodded his thanks. "And yours as well. But we carry on. It is what they would have wanted. My father left his doctor's practice to me, and I intend to see it flourish. What did your father want for you?"

"He wanted me to come to Wakefield," Heather said, "and learn all I could. Book learning, and work too. About the textiles industry."

"Then it would be an honour to him if you did just that," Dr. Armstrong said.

Heather nodded, but her stomach twisted at his words, the pain of Aunt Ida's neglect striking her once again. Her father had wanted her to receive a good education, but she did not believe now that Aunt Ida ever truly intended to provide one. Heather was free labour to her, and little more.

But, Heather thought, she had to make the best of it now, for her father's sake. If she worked hard and did all that Aunt Ida asked, perhaps her education would come in time. And if it did not, at least Aunt Ida had access to books, and to acquaintances like Dr. Armstrong. She could educate herself in every free moment she could find, and honour her father's hopes that way.

"Are you in a rush, Dr. Armstrong?" she asked him softly.

He looked surprised. "No," he said. "In fact, I have just finished work for the day."

"Would you join me on my walk?" she asked, shyly. "I'm not sure I want to be alone."

He hesitated for a moment, and then smiled and offered her a small bow. "It would be my pleasure, Miss Green," he said.

CHAPTER NINE

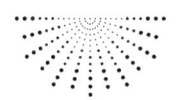

Heather walked the city streets with Dr. Armstrong, and she found herself telling him about her papa and their life in Grimsby. Aunt Ida did not like Heather talking about her old life, as she claimed it showed how uncouth her niece really was, but Heather could not stop the words pouring out to Dr. Armstrong's sympathetic ear now. She told him about going fishing together on the boat, and about their morning drinks from Mrs. Atha's, and Old Jenny's double helping of gossip and stew at the market. She even told him the story of how her father had found her in his fishing boat all those years ago, and how no one knew where she came from, really, but how everyone said that she came from the sea itself, as a blessing for her father.

"It sounds like he loved you very much," Dr. Armstrong commented, and Heather's heart swelled to think that that, at least, was true.

They met a few more times after that, and slowly Dr. Armstrong began to open up to Heather about his own life and past. He was a general surgeon at St. Mark Voluntary Hospital, but he had recently taken over his father's practice too, and he worried, in his darker moments, that he would not be able to live up to his father's legacy. He worried his father's patients saw him as too young and inexperienced, and that the work his father had dedicated his life to would fade away.

"I don't think that can be true," Heather said softly. "You are a wonderful doctor."

"Thank you, Miss Green," he said. "I am glad you think so."

After a week, however, Aunt Ida's worries for her nieces faded, and she returned to tyrannical form. No one had cleaned the house while Heather had been ill, so Heather had extra cleaning to do now, as well as her shifts at the factory. She missed the fresh air of her walks, as well as Dr. Armstrong's company, but Aunt Ida's schedule left her with no time for leisure, and now that her father was gone, Heather had to please her aunt more than ever. Aunt Ida never missed an opportunity to tell Heather that she was fed and housed by her aunt's generosity alone, and the unspoken threat over what would happen if Heather became unsatisfactory loomed in Heather's thoughts every day.

Still, she remembered her promise to her father, and she stole what moments she could to study by herself. School seemed an impossible dream now, but if that ever changed, she wanted to be ready.

Heather was sixteen when she saw Dr. Armstrong again. She was cleaning the kitchen, trying to ignore the throbbing in her head from lack of sleep, when she heard a panicked gasp from her aunt upstairs. Heather ran after the sound, and she found her aunt collapsed on the floor in the living room, clutching her chest with one hand. Her aunt gaped at her like a fish out of water, and Heather looked at her for barely a second before she turned and ran.

"What is going on?" Edna asked, as she descended the stairs.

"Aunt Ida is ill," Heather said. "We need to fetch a doctor, quickly."

Heather tore through town, as fast as her feet could carry her, and skidded to a halt in front of Dr. Armstrong's practice. His name shone on a shiny bronze plaque on the door, and Heather scurried up the steps, desperately praying that he would be available to help.

He answered the door himself, and he seemed startled by Heather's appearance. "Miss Green," he said, and Heather was surprised then too, because she had been certain he would not remember her. "Whatever is the matter?"

"My aunt," she said, breathlessly. "She collapsed. Something's very wrong."

"I'll come at once," Dr. Armstrong said.

Dr. Armstrong's diagnosis was better than Heather had thought, but not as good as she would have hoped. Aunt Ida had suffered a mild heart attack, and she needed rest and quiet to recuperate. He provided a tonic to help sooth Aunt Ida's nerves, and assured her that although the danger was past this time, she needed to be careful about how she exerted herself from now on.

Aunt Ida was so grateful to him, and so fearful for her own health, that she insisted he return daily to offer his advice until Aunt Ida was well enough to rise from bed again.

Heather knew it was wicked to find any bright element to her aunt's illness, but she felt that her life became significantly lighter in its aftermath. With Aunt Ida confined to her bedchambers, Heather could work without fearing Aunt Ida's displeased comments or punishments. Aunt Ida was too tired to judge Heather's work, so Heather got a full portion of food every night, and the cook snuck her some extra snacks as well. Aunt Ida could not bear to be in the house alone, and she did not trust Edna to raise a finger to help her, so Heather was not expected to work at the factory until her aunt had recovered.

The only downside for Heather, perhaps, was the increased time she spent in her aunt's company, as her aunt constantly rang the bell with demands and was often desperate enough for a companion that she insisted Heather stay and read to her. Even these moments had their upsides, however. Heather was allowed to get off her feet, and she was able to read, not in the dead of night by candlelight but in a bright, sunny room.

And of course, Dr. Armstrong was in her life again. He visited every day for that first week, and maintained regular visits even after Aunt Ida was back on her feet. Aunt Ida was terrified that she would fall ill again, and so she insisted on seeing Dr. Armstrong once a week, so he could listen to her heart and reassure her that all was well.

Heather had little opportunity to speak with Dr. Armstrong during these visits, but they always exchanged smiles and friendly greetings, and he would enquire after her health in a tone that sounded less like the question of a doctor and more like the question of a friend. Heather greatly admired Dr. Armstrong's kind approach to someone as difficult and finicky as her aunt, and she began to desperately look forward to his visits, and to the smiles and hellos they would provide.

Matthew was always at the factory, so he had no opinions on the doctor either way, but his wife Edna seemed taken with him as well. She would find excuses to be home during his visits, and would elbow Heather out of the way to answer the door when he called and show him to her aunt. She would touch his arm gently as they talked, and she spoke in a softer voice than Heather had ever heard her use before, her tone always light and cheery.

"Thank you ever so much for all your attentions to my mother-in-law," Edna said to him, as she walked him to the door after one of his visits. "You are too kind to us." She raised her hand to brush his arm, smiling, and Dr. Armstrong nodded politely in response.

"I'm just doing my job, Mrs. Owens."

"Well, it is always a pleasure to see your handsome face," Edna said.

Dr. Armstrong gave her a polite bow in response, and then turned to Heather, who had also followed them down the stairs. "Good afternoon, Miss Green," he said. "I look forward to seeing you again soon."

"Good afternoon, Dr. Armstrong," she said softly, and he smiled at her. The exchange was short, but as soon as Dr. Armstrong had gone from the house, Edna whirled on Heather, all her sweetness gone.

"Do you really think he could care for you?" she asked. "A little fishergirl like you?"

"I'm sorry?" Heather asked. "What do you mean?"

"I mean," Edna said sharply, "that I saw the way you looked at him, how you smiled at him. It was unseemly. If you think a handsome doctor like that would take an interest in a girl like you, you are sorely mistaken."

Heather felt herself blushing. Was her affection really so obvious? She had no illusions about herself or her relationship with Dr. Armstrong, but she enjoyed seeing him. She felt a surprising warmth in her chest when he looked at her, and if polite greetings were all she would ever get from him, she was happy to receive them, but now she felt uncertain. Was she behaving improperly by liking him?

"Dr. Armstrong is a family friend," she said. "Of course I am polite to him."

"That look on your face was not politeness," Edna said. "And the look he gave you wasn't politeness either."

"What look?" Heather asked, but she felt like she knew. Dr. Armstrong did have a certain kindness and softness on his face when he looked at her and bid her goodbye, but Heather had assumed it was just his general kind demeanour, and nothing more.

"He wouldn't marry you, you know," Edna said haughtily. "Whatever he tells you. He has ambitions and tastes that are far superior to you."

"I never thought he would marry me," Heather said softly, and Edna raised her eyebrows.

"Then your behaviour is even more objectionable. Mother

will be furious when she hears, after all she has done for you."

"What behaviour?" Heather asked. "I haven't done anything except greet him and bid him farewell. Surely Aunt Ida would be more upset if I *didn't* do that."

Edna rolled her eyes. "You are a naive, foolish thing, aren't you? No wonder he's taken such an interest in you."

Heather wanted to argue what Edna had said, not moments ago, that Dr. Armstrong could never take a real interest in her, but she thought it would be better not to argue. Edna was in a fury about something, and although Heather was certain she had done nothing wrong, it would not be wise to provoke her.

Edna's accusations were still in Heather's thoughts when she encountered Dr. Armstrong near the market the following day. He bowed at her and tipped his hat, inquiring after her health and her business in town, and she smiled a little tentatively back at him, and answered in kind.

They were heading in the same direction, so they began to walk side by side. "I want to thank you," Heather said as they walked, "for taking such good care of my aunt. I know she is not always an easy woman."

"I must make a confession," Dr. Armstrong said. "Your aunt has not needed my help for some time, although she does not believe it. But I have not tried to convince her as much as I should, perhaps, because I greatly enjoy the opportunity to see you."

Heather blushed and looked at the ground, but she could not stop herself smiling. "Is that true?" she asked softly.

"Very much so," he said. "Your smile is the highlight of my week."

"Then I will try to smile more often, sir," she said.

"Please," he said. "Call me David. If you would like."

Heather felt a delighted shiver run up her spine. "Alright," she said. "David then. And you must call me Heather. If *you* would like."

"Heather," he said with a smile and a respectful nod, and as Heather looked at his expression out of the corner of her eye, she knew that both she and Edna had been wrong. Dr. Armstrong, David, seemed to care for her very much, and Heather could no longer deny that she cared for him too.

CHAPTER TEN

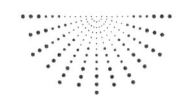

After that, Edna always found an excuse to send Heather out of the house when David Armstrong paid his visits. Heather could not object to the chance to get extra fresh air, but she missed seeing David's face. With time to think on it, Heather wondered if perhaps Edna was jealous of the friendship between the pair. She did not understand *why* Edna would be jealous, when she was a married woman with many friends. She never needed to lift a finger at home or at the factory, and everyone seemed to like despite her rudeness, but it seemed the only reasonable explanation. Edna did not want David preferring Heather over her, and so she made sure Heather was always out of sight.

Heather desperately longed to see him again, but her outings never brought them together, and it seemed far too forward to call on him without a medical necessity to precipitate it.

But finally, after several weeks, she saw David again while she was at the market. She hurried over to him, beaming. "David!" she said.

He looked up at her shout, but he did not smile. "Miss Green," he said, and he nodded politely. "Good afternoon."

She continued to move towards him, but he did not stop his own stride, and soon he had passed her and was continuing up the street out of sight. Heather stared after him, feeling perplexed. Never once had he been so cold to her before. It was as though their last conversation, indeed, their entire acquaintance, had been forgotten.

It worried her, but she tried to reassure herself as she went about her day. David was a very busy man, with many patients to care for. He held life and death in his hands. If he was in a rush, it was for a very good reason, something so compelling that he could not even risk the time to pause and explain. Next time she saw him, she thought, he would apologise for his brusqueness, and all would be well.

Still, Heather was troubled by what she had seen, and she could not bear to wait until they met by accident in town again. What if he was just as busy a second time? When Edna made excuses to get Heather out of the house during David's next visit, Heather worked as quickly as she could, buying vegetables at the market without even looking at them, and then racing back to the house. She knew she risked being punished for her carelessness, but her heart would not rest until she saw David again.

She entered the hallway just as David was collecting his hat to depart. Edna was with him, smiling at him, and he smiled politely back at her.

"Dr. Armstrong," Heather said, not wishing to use his first name in front of Edna.

David looked up, but the smile slid from his face. "Miss Green," he said. "Good day to you."

"Good day, sir," Heather said softly, and with a bow to Edna, Dr. Armstrong strode from the house.

"It seems he doesn't like you all that much after all," Edna said, smiling. "What a pity."

Heather whirled on Edna, anger rising within her. "What did you do?" she asked.

"I simply spoke to him," Edna said, with a careless shrug.

"What did you say?"

"The truth," Edna said. "That you are a money-hungry little thing, and lazy too. I told him how mother despairs of you, such a flirt as you are, risking the reputation of this family with your behaviour. Of course, we keep you here, because we hope you will find improvement, and you have nowhere else to go, but mother is truly at her wit's end."

"And he believed you?" Heather asked. Her stomach felt like lead.

"Why would he not?" Edna replied. "Mother spoke to him too. She noticed your behaviour as well, it seems, and she wanted to warn Dr. Armstrong not to be taken in by your charms, because you are deceitful and manipulative and she does not want to see him trapped in your web."

Tears stung Heather's eyes. "Why would you do that?" she whispered.

"I told you, Heather," Edna said. "He could never truly care for you. Now you see it too."

Edna sauntered away, and Heather leaned back against the wall, blinded by her tears. It was not even really that she had cared for David and had thought he cared for her in return, at least not in that way. It was that, for the first time in years, she had had a friend, and Edna had torn him away from her. It did not matter what Heather said or did now, after Edna had called her manipulative and a liar. David's opinion was set against her now, and no words from Heather would convince him otherwise.

She wiped her eyes furiously with the back of her hand. Crying would not help the situation, but she felt helpless.

Dr. Armstrong continued his weekly visits, and he greeted Heather with the same cool politeness every time. Edna no longer worked to keep Heather out of the house, now that her scheme had been successful, and instead she delighted in pulling David into conversation in front of Heather and forcing Heather to see how cool and distant he continued to be.

After a time, Dr. Armstrong gave Aunt Ida a full bill of health, and his visits to the house slowed, although they did not end completely. Heather was back to working at the factory, and the hope she had found during Aunt Ida's illness vanished. She began to feel that her entire life would be spent in Aunt Ida's service, toiling at the factory and cleaning the house without a penny of pay and no chance to ever leave.

CHAPTER ELEVEN

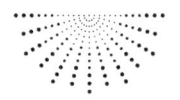

Things changed again when Heather was seventeen, but not for the better. Matthew was involved in an accident in the factory, and his resulting broken leg caused him to spend several days at home, while Aunt Ida ran the factory in his stead.

Heather had very few encounters with Matthew in the four years she had lived in Wakefield. When she had first moved into the house, at thirteen, Matthew had treated her with about as much significance as he treated a fly that had flown in through the window, and his glances were fleeting and dismissive. As she had grown, however, Heather had noticed Matthew's gaze lingering on her longer, taking in the details of her form. Matthew was still at the factory most hours of the day, and he lounged with Edna when he was home, so Heather still hardly ever encountered him, but she knew he was aware of her in a way he had not been before.

After the accident, Matthew insisted on being waited on hand and foot, and although Edna kept him company, she was certainly not going to scurry back and forth to fetch him food or books at his request. So, for the first time, Heather found herself frequently summoned into Matthew's presence.

She loathed it. Matthew's eyes lingered on her in a way that felt entirely improper, and he began to make little comments to her as she scurried back and forth, telling her what a pretty little thing she was and asking how grateful she was to be indebted to his family. Heather's skin crawled at just the thought of his eyes on her, but she had nowhere else to go, and she knew Aunt Ida would not take kindly to any accusations against her son. All Heather could do was work as quickly as she could manage in his presence, and then depart before he had too much time to speak.

Heather hoped that things would improve once Matthew recovered and returned to the factory, but if anything, they got worse. While Matthew's leg was injured, he could only look at Heather, and she made sure to give him a wide berth and stay out of arm's reach. Once his leg was better and he was able to walk again, he was in the house less, but he still called Heather into his presence often, and he would grab at her every chance he got. Heather grew to fear being alone with him, knowing that she had nothing more than her wits to protect herself from his advances.

It seemed ironic, she thought, that Edna had driven a good man like David away from Heather with rumours of impropriety, when Edna's husband was the real threat in that regard.

Heather knew no-one else in the house would believe her if she told them. All she could do was avoid Matthew and hope that he got bored in time.

For a while, that strategy seemed to work. Demand at the factory increased, so both she and Matthew were working longer hours at opposite ends of the building. Heather had also turned eighteen, and the milestone offered distracting new concerns. Aunt Ida had always referred to Heather as her young ward, but that story could not last forever. It was one thing for a thirteen year old to live with her great aunt in the name of an education. It was quite another for a grown woman to do so. Under normal circumstances, of course, Heather might be considered a guest of her aunt's until she married. But she knew now that Edna and Aunt Ida had no intention of allowing Heather to find such happiness. They would work her until she was no longer useful, and then she could not imagine what would happen to her. Turning eighteen felt like a milestone on that path, a point where Aunt Ida might officially make her a servant or send her off alone, guilt-free.

David still made occasional visits to the house, but Heather avoided him. She could not bear to see how coldly he looked at her, or to remember the lies that Edna and Aunt Ida had told. Yet the thought of David in the house was distracting at best, heart-breaking at worst, and Heather found it very difficult to get any work done knowing he was close.

After one such visit from the doctor, Aunt Ida and Edna went out to visit friends, leaving Heather behind to clean. Heather was distracted, her thoughts on the doctor, and from there leading her to muse on memories of her father, and how she and David had first bonded immediately after his death.

She was so wrapped up in her own thoughts that she did not notice Matthew in the hallway by the stairs until she almost walked into him. She gasped in surprise and flinched back as he gripped her arms to hold them both steady.

"I'm sorry, sir," she said. "I didn't know you were home."

Matthew grinned at her. "I needed a break from the factory," he said. "And we've had so little chance to be alone together, haven't we?"

Heather tried to step back, to increase the space between them, but Matthew's hands dug into the flesh of her arms, holding her in place.

"Please, sir," Heather said. "I need to finish my work."

"Oh, I think that can wait, don't you?" Matthew said. He stepped forward, crowding Heather until she was forced to move with him, her back landing against the side of the stairs. "I've seen you, girl. Watching me. Admiring me when my wife isn't looking. You always look so lonely."

"No, sir," Heather said, shaking her head. "Please."

"It's indecent," he said. "You being here, looking the way you do, looking at me the way you do. Something needs to be done about it, wouldn't you agree?"

Heather shook her head harder, struggling to escape from his grip.

"We're alone now, Heather," he said, in a low voice. "Just you and me. I think it's time we got to know each other."

He grabbed Heather by the shoulders now and pressed his lips to hers in a brutal kiss. Heather screamed and pushed against his chest as hard as she could, struggling with all her might. His grip loosened for a second, and she tried to run around him to escape, but then he struck her face with the back of his hand, and she staggered to the floor from the blow.

Her lip felt like it was swelling up instantly, and the entire side of her face was on fire from the force of his attack. Heather scrambled to her hands and knees, fighting to crawl away, but Matthew was upon her, grabbing at her arms and pulling at her clothes. Her dress ripped, and Heather screamed again. He put a hand over her mouth, and she bit him as hard as she could, flailing and fighting to escape.

Distantly, she heard a gasp, and then a shout. "What is the meaning of this?"

It was Aunt Ida. Matthew sprang away from Heather instantly, leaving her crying and gasping for breath on the ground, her skirt and bodice both ripped and bruises blooming on her face and arms.

Aunt Ida and Edna stood in the doorway, home early from their outing. Both stared at Matthew and Heather with fury in their eyes.

Heather staggered to her feet, clutching the bodice of her dress, as Edna strode towards her. "You little slut!" she shouted. "Going after Dr. Armstrong wasn't enough? You also had to try and steal my husband?"

"I didn't," Heather said, through her sobs. "I didn't want--"

"I have never seen such disgraceful behaviour in all my days," Aunt Ida said. "And in the hallway of this house!" Her gaze was still fixed on Heather. "I knew you were a despicable girl, but even I never thought you would sink this low."

"He attacked me!" Heather shouted. "I didn't do anything."

"She propositioned me, mother," Matthew said. "She has been doing so for weeks. I tried to tell her that I was married, that I wasn't interested in a thing like her, but she would not take no for an answer."

"That isn't true!" Heather said. The world spun slightly around her from the force of Matthew's blow, and she struggled to stand upright, but she had to fight for herself. "Look at me, Aunt Ida. He hit me. He tore my dress. Please."

Aunt Ida looked down her nose at Heather, her eyes narrowed, and she sniffed. "I do not think my son is a liar," she said. "You, on the other hand, well, I suppose it is in your blood. How dare you tempt my son? How dare you try to corrupt him with your loose morals, after all that we have done for you?"

Heather shook her head, but Aunt Ida was not listening to her now. "I want you out of this house," Aunt Ida said. "At once. You have tainted this family for too long."

"No!" Heather said desperately. "Please." She did not want to stay anywhere near Matthew, but she had no other family or friends, and not a penny to her name. She could not bear to imagine what would happen to her if she was thrown out on the street. "I have nowhere else to go."

"Then go to the workhouse," Aunt Ida said. "Maybe you will learn a work ethic and some morals there. But get out of my house." She marched forward and grabbed Heather by the bruised arm, and Heather swallowed a cry of pain. Aunt Ida hauled her to the door.

"But my things," Heather said. "My clothes."

"I purchased them," Aunt Ida said. "They are *my* things." She threw Heather out of the door, and Heather stumbled down the steps, the world still spinning around her. "Do not dare show your face here again, or I will be forced to call the police."

"Aunt Ida!" Heather said, but Aunt Ida slammed the door in her face, leaving Heather out on the streets, sick, penniless and alone.

CHAPTER TWELVE

Heather did not dare to linger on the doorstep, but she also could not bear to wander into the centre of town, looking as she did. She stumbled away from the house and the factory, following the flow of the river. Once she was out of sight of the factory, she sat down on the bank, pressed her forehead against her knees, and wept.

She did not know how long she stayed there, but it was growing dark and cold by the time she stopped crying and looked up. She was terrified to stay out here all night by herself, but she truly had nowhere else to go. Would it really be the workhouse for her? Once she ended up in there, she did not think she would ever escape it again. But could it really be so much worse than life with Aunt Ida, working all day every day, and getting hardly any food or rest?

Yes, she thought forlornly. It could be worse. At least Matthew had only been one threat. The workhouse was full of men like him, supervisors who might prey upon the helplessness of the women forced under their watchful eyes.

Sadly, she did not think she had a choice.

Heather was just steeling herself to stand and move on when she heard a shout down the path, from the direction of the factory. "Miss Green? Is that you?"

Heather spun around. A woman was walking down the canal path towards her. It was difficult to see in the dark, and at first Heather could not place the voice. Then the woman moved closer, and Heather recognised her. Her name was Madge Canning, and she was a woman in her forties who worked at Matthew and Aunt Ida's factory. Heather had hardly ever spoken to her, as it would be impossible to do so over the roar of the machines all day and night, but she knew her as a hardworking woman, and a generally kind one.

"Miss Green!" Mrs. Canning said. "What are you doing out here all alone?"

Heather tried to respond, but the moment she opened her mouth to speak, she broke down into sobs again.

"Oh, dear," Mrs. Canning said. She hurried the rest of the distance and knelt down beside Heather. "Oh, dear, now. It's all right. You're all right. What's happened, my love?"

"My Aunt Ida kicked me out," Heather said, through her sobs. "Her son, Matthew, Mr. Owens, he thought we were alone in the house, and he *attacked* me. He bruised my face and tore my dress. But when his mother came home, she said that I had-- that I had--" It was too awful to speak aloud, but Mrs. Canning seemed to understand. She wrapped an arm around Heather and pulled her close.

"There, there, now," she said. "It's all right."

Heather shook her head. "No," she said. "Aunt Ida said she would call the police if I came back, and I don't know what lies she would tell about me, but I'm certain they'd believe her over me. And I have nowhere to go. My father died, and I have no other relatives, and no friends here. What am I going to do?"

"Shush," Mrs. Canning said. "Don't worry about all that just now. You've been through a very difficult day. I'm just glad I chose to take the canal path home today. And you're lucky, too. There can be some rough sorts around here at night. Come on," she added, standing up and holding out a hand to Heather. "Let's get you safe inside. My house isn't too far from here. I'll make us some stew."

"Oh, no," Heather said. "I couldn't impose."

"It's not imposing if I invite you," Mrs. Canning said. "And I want you to come. I'm certainly not going to leave you sitting out here, am I? Come on then."

Heather nodded, and allowed Mrs. Canning to lead her away down the river.

Mrs. Canning lived in a small terraced house about a mile away from the factory with her son, Trevor. "But don't you worry yourself about him," Mrs. Canning said. "He's an excellent lad, and he's out of town right now anyway, so I've got plenty of room for you." The house itself was a little cluttered and cramped, but it was warm and dry, and Mrs. Canning's gentle voice made it feel as cosy as a feather bed and as safe as being at home with her papa. Heather sat at the kitchen table while her hostess prepared a stew for them. She expected her to ask more questions about the incident, but she chattered on about inconsequential things, telling Heather about a pain she'd been getting in her wrist and about the gossip she gathered from all around town in her work as a seamstress.

"The factory's not bad," Mrs. Canning said. "There are worse ones, certainly. But the money isn't enough. I always try and do a bit of mending in the evenings, once I come back here." She glanced at Heather's torn dress. "Let me get you something else to wear, and I'll fix that up for you as well."

Heather still did not wish to impose, but she was too tired to resist. Mrs. Canning lent her one of her own nightgowns, and the pair of them sat by the fireside with a basket of Mrs. Canning's mending beside them.

"It's all right," Heather said, when she saw just how much work Mrs. Canning had to do. "I can mend it, if you can spare a needle and thread."

"Alright then," Mrs. Canning said, and the two of them fell into companionable silence as they both worked. Heather kept her eyes fixed on the sewing, focusing on every stitch as though the movement of the needle could erase the memories of the day from her mind. Mrs. Canning watched her too.

"You're quite handy with a needle," she said, once Heather was done. Mrs.. Canning held out her hand for the garment, and when Heather handed it over, she inspected the sewing with narrowed eyes. "Good quality stitching, hardly noticeable at all."

"My father was a fisherman," Heather said softly. "There were often things that needed fixing, and you learn to be quick with your hands on the sea. And the past few years, my Aunt Ida has had me doing the mending for her, whenever anything got worn through."

"You said your father died?" Mrs. Canning asked her.

Heather nodded. "He had an accident," she said. "At sea. He sent me to my aunt's to get an education, but I'm sure this isn't how he imagined things."

"No," Mrs. Canning said. "I think you're right there. Still, this is good work." She handed the dress back, frowning.

"Perhaps you could help me with some of this," she said. "I can pay you for it."

"Oh, no," Heather said. "I couldn't possibly accept any money from you. You've already helped me enough. But I'm happy to sew with you, if you'd like me to."

Mrs. Canning gave her a shrewd look. "You shouldn't turn down money, girl. After all that's happened, you're still too sweet for this world, by the sounds of it. But if that's the way you want things, I won't argue with you. Try this gentleman's shirt first, then. There's a small tear just by the cuff."

They spent the rest of the evening working together, and Mrs. Canning asked Heather no further questions about her past or the events of the day. Eventually, both the fire and the candles had burnt low, and Mrs. Canning suggested they retire to sleep. Heather could use her son's room, she said, since he had been out of town for a while. "Clean sheets and everything," Mrs. Canning said, as she handed Heather a candle stub.

Heather whispered her thanks and scurried up to bed. There was a jug of water on the cabinet in the bedroom, and she splashed her face with it before daring to look in the glass beside her. Her lip was twice the size it normally was, with a dramatic split in the corner, and the area around her right eye and cheek had turned purple. The rest of her skin looked unnaturally pale, and her eyes were red from crying. No wonder Mrs. Canning had stopped and insisted on bring her home, Heather thought. She looked broken.

She felt broken, too, as she climbed into bed and blew out the candle. All her limbs ached from the struggle against Matthew, but the physical pain was nothing compared to the pain in her heart. Every time she tried to close her eyes, images of Matthew bearing down on her flashed through her mind, and Heather's chest grew tight at the memory, making it difficult to breathe. She had not really trusted Aunt Ida to help her, of course. If she had, she would have spoken to her about Matthew's behaviour long ago. But it was still shocking, still horrifying, to see her aunt take in her bruised, torn, bloodied form, and dismiss the idea of an attack outright. She must have known, in her heart, that Matthew had assaulted her niece, and that all his words were lies, but even with the evidence before her, she would not accept it, and now Heather was alone.

Well, not quite alone, Heather thought, every time her racing heart felt too much for her. There were still kind people in the world, and she had friends that she had not even realised she had. For this night, at least, she had Mrs. Canning on her side. She would figure out the rest of it when she awoke.

CHAPTER THIRTEEN

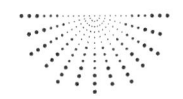

Mrs. Canning left early for her factory shift the following morning, but she told Heather she could remain in her house and get some rest. Heather could not bear the stillness, and she hated the idea of being a burden on her rescuer, and so she worked hard all day, putting Aunt Ida's lessons to good use, cleaning, tidying, and preparing a simple meal for dinner.

Mrs. Canning seemed delighted when she returned home, and when Heather tried to excuse herself and leave for the evening, Mrs. Canning insisted that she stay the night again. They spent another evening sewing together. Before the fireplace flickered out and they retired for the night, Mrs. Canning spoke.

"How are you doing today, my dear?" she asked. Heather could not think how to answer that in words, so she simply nodded. "You are a brave girl," Mrs. Canning said. "You've been through a lot, and yet here you still are." She did another couple of stitches, seeming to consider her next words. "I don't like to think of you headed to the workhouse," she said. "And I certainly don't want you out on the street either. You've a good hand for mending, anyone could see that. Why don't you stay here and work with me a little while?"

"Work with you?" Heather asked.

Mrs. Canning nodded. "I get more mending work than I can manage while still working at the factory, and not enough to quit working there, and I'd say your stitching is as solid as mine. If you do some of the mending work for me, I could pay you for the trouble, and you can stay here as well, as long as you need to."

"You would pay me?" Heather asked, with awe in her voice. She would have worked just for the roof over her head. The idea of someone paying her was foreign to her.

"Of course I would pay you," Mrs. Canning said. "I'm no crook. You're a good girl, Heather, in a bad spot. I want to help you out. But don't go thinking this is charity. I can't afford charity. Your work is good, and I need the help, so I'll pay you for your work and we'll keep each other company while my son is away. Does that sound fair?"

"Yes, Mrs. Canning," Heather said, tears forming in her eyes. "Thank you."

"Well, none of that, if you're staying," Mrs. Canning said. "Call me Madge."

They fell back into working silently again, but Heather's mind buzzed with thoughts. She could not have dreamed of a better opportunity. With that sort of work, she might be able to support herself one day, and if Madge Canning paid her for the work she did now, Heather would have money of her own for the first time since she left for Wakefield. She immediately started wondering how much the train fare to Grimsby might cost. It had been four years since her father's death, and she still had not been able to visit his grave. Perhaps if she could do that, some of the pain of the loss might begin to ease.

Madge could not pay her much, of course, on top of housing her, but Heather was incredibly grateful for all she received, and she cleaned the house while Madge was at work as well as helping with the mending. The only chore she did not do was going to the market, or really anything that required leaving the house. Her nights were plagued by nightmares about Matthew and Aunt Ida, and she was terrified of encountering them in town. She did not know what they thought had become of her, but she imagined them snatching her by the arm and dragging her away if they ever found her, forcing her back into servitude at the house or hauling her to the police station with a false report of a crime. Madge worried at her young guest's reluctance to leave the house, but work kept them both so busy that she did not press the issue.

About a month after Heather's arrival, Madge received a letter. "It's from my son," she told Heather by the fireside that night. "I told you he's been away, working in Liverpool. Well, the factory he was working at is being sold, and a friend offered him a job as a foreman in a factory here. Quite a promotion! So he'll be back as soon as he can."

Heather bit her lip. "If you need me to leave-" she began, but Madge cut her off.

"Goodness, no," she said. "I don't mean that at all. I'm certain he'll want to find a place of his own soon enough, without his mother watching over him. And until then, you can share my room with me, if you don't mind it."

"I don't mind it at all," Heather said. "Thank you."

"I should be the one thanking you," Madge said. "Demand for our sewing has gone up since you moved here, and it's wonderful to have someone to talk to in the evenings. My son was never such good company. I have half a mind to make him sleep in the kitchen and keep that room for you. But I won't, don't you worry," she added. "I've got rather a vested interest in you and Trevor getting along." She winked at Heather, and Heather found herself blushing.

She could not admit it to Madge, but she was nervous about the thought of her son coming home and staying with them. Nightmares of Matthew still haunted her, and she was not certain if she could trust any man not to hurt her. Even wonderful, kind-hearted David had thrown her aside based on gossip and rumours that he could not have truly believed. She had confided her secrets in him. He had known her better than anybody living, and he had still turned away from her the moment the opportunity presented itself.

She had not realised, when she was a girl, how special her papa truly was, for loving her completely, even without knowing a thing about where she came from, even without there being any connection between them by blood. She had loved him, of course, and appreciated his love for her, but she had not realised just how special his love was, just how truly blessed she had been, until it was gone and could never return.

More bad news came in the following days, although Heather tried to pretend her indifference. Madge often shared gossip from the families she worked for in the evenings, and Heather was just mildly nodding along to the discussion of Mrs. Thomas's daughter's new engagement, until Madge mentioned the name of the groom. "Dr. David Armstrong, he is," Madge said.

Heather's hand jolted, driving the needle into her finger. "David Armstrong?" she repeated, as she put her finger to her mouth to stop the bleeding. It couldn't be, she thought.

But then, why not? He no longer had any care or affection for her, and it had been over a year since he last looked at her with any kindness. Why would he not be getting married to a sophisticated, well-to-do girl, the sort that Heather could never be? She had not been good enough for him, just as Edna had so cruelly told her. His affection for her had never meant much. She was silly to even dwell on it now.

"That's what I heard," Madge said. "Well, I've never met him myself, but a doctor at such a young age must be an excellent catch for a young girl, mustn't he?"

"Yes," Heather said distractedly. "I'm sure he must."

"Are you all right, Heather, dear?" Madge asked her, pausing in her sewing. "You've turned rather pale."

"I'm just tired," Heather said. "It's been quite a long day."

Madge did not press her any further, but Heather knew she was not convinced, and Madge avoided mentioning Dr. David Armstrong or his upcoming nuptials again.

CHAPTER FOURTEEN

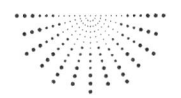

The day of Madge's son Trevor's return arrived, and Madge and Heather both worked to prepare a miniature feast for the occasion. Heather was still more than a little nervous about his appearance, but she assured herself that she could trust Madge, so if Madge said he was a good person, then a good person he had to be. Aunt Ida had never cared for Heather's well-being, except when it directly affected her ability to work. Madge was different, and so Trevor would be different too.

Still, when a loud knock sounded on the front door that evening and Madge jumped to her feet shouting, "He's here!" Heather could not stop her hands from shaking a little. Madge opened the door to reveal a tall, round-faced young man smiling broadly.

"Mother!" he said, as she enveloped him in a hug.

"Trevor," she said. "It's so good to see you. I'm glad you're home at last."

"I was only in Liverpool, Mother," Trevor said, good-naturedly. "You make it sound like I went off to war."

"What difference does it make whether it was Liverpool or China," Madge said, "when you were too far away for me to visit either way?" She hugged him again. "My goodness, you've grown."

Trevor laughed. "Mother, I haven't grown a bit for the last four or five years."

"Then maybe I've shrunk," Madge laughed. "I don't remember you being this tall." She stepped aside for her son to enter the kitchen and helped him remove his coat and hat. Then he noticed Heather.

"Hullo," he said. "I don't believe we've met. I'm Trevor Canning. I suppose you must know my mother."

"Trevor," Madge said, "this is the friend I told you about. She's been staying with me for a few weeks now, and her sewing work is like a dream."

"It's a pleasure to make your acquaintance, miss," Trevor said.

"And you as well," Heather said. He seemed friendly, at least. Matthew had never seemed warm or welcoming in all the time she had known him, so this was a solid point of difference between them, at least.

"Well, come in, come in," Madge said, even though her son had already removed his hat and closed the front door behind him. "We've prepared a feast to celebrate. All your favourites."

"Thank you," Trevor said, as his mother guided him to the table. "And thanks especially to you, miss. You didn't need to do anything for me."

Heather murmured something vague about it being quite all right, but even she could not have said exactly what that was. She said as little as possible during the meal, but she took the opportunity to study Trevor's face. He had the same eyes and nose as his mother, and his hair had a wildness to it that reminded her of Madge as well, but his height must have come from his father. He ate heartily, with many compliments to his mother's cooking, and then retired, claiming exhaustion from the long journey. Once he had gone to bed, Madge and Heather settled by the fire to do some mending, and Madge turned the conversation once again to her son.

"He must have grown," she said. "He looks so much taller. Don't you think he looks tall?"

"Very tall," Heather agreed.

"He's a good, strong lad," Madge said, "and so polite too. I always insisted that manners are important, but then, not much insisting was required. He's always cared about others almost more than he cares about himself."

Heather nodded as she chattered, unable to contribute much to the conversation. She had to admit that Trevor did seem kind-hearted, as his mother said. But these days, she found it difficult to trust anybody outside of Madge herself, and even that trust was tentative and hard won.

Life was different with Trevor around, but Heather was unsure whether that was a bad thing. Trevor worked all day, as Madge did, leaving Heather to sew and care for the house, but he left before his mother in the morning and returned home a little before her at night, leaving about half an hour of time where they were alone, with Heather cooking and Trevor reading the newspaper at the kitchen table and talking idly about his day.

At first, this arrangement made Heather nervous. The idea of being alone with any man was frightening, after what had happened with Matthew, and even if Trevor had no such intentions towards her, she knew it was generally considered improper for a young unmarried man and a young unmarried woman to be in a house together alone for any length of time. She almost wondered if she would be better off taking a walk at that time every day, to save them both the embarrassment and anxiety, but then who would prepare dinner for when Madge returned? Madge had given her so much, and making sure she always had a hot meal at the end of the day was the least that Heather could do in return.

But slowly, Heather grew to accept and even appreciate Trevor's presence. He always looked tired when he returned home from work, but he greeted her with a smile as he hung up his hat, and always enquired after her day with a cheery kindness that went far beyond common courtesy. As he read the newspaper, he would comment about current events, muttering about the politicians or exclaiming about the exciting new discoveries of the British Empire, and although Heather knew little about these topics at first, it felt good to be included. For the first time, she thought, she was actually learning like her father had wished, but it was a factory foreman and his newspaper, not a rich great aunt and a fancy school, that provided it.

Trevor often asked Heather's opinion, and although she demurred at first, she soon found that she liked being asked what she thought. Trevor had strong views of his own, about the importance of trade unions, about workers' rights and a man's need to be represented in his government, and Heather found that she admired the fire in him as he spoke. He was a strange combination of calm kindness and fierce conviction, and the more Heather got to know him, the more she appreciated it.

Once Madge returned from work, they would all eat at the kitchen table together, the newspaper and politics folded away. Trevor would usually retire soon after dinner, but sometimes he would sit up in the living room while Madge and Heather sewed by the fire, listening to his mother's gossip and offering far more of a smiling commentary than Heather could ever provide. She did not know most of the people Madge gossiped about, but Trevor had been familiar with the city and its people since birth, and he was excellent at providing his mother with just the right reaction to gratify her, while explaining a bit more of the context of the joke to Heather as he did.

Slowly, Heather worked up the courage to leave the house, as long as she avoided the factory and the centre of town. Mostly, she stuck to the country paths, roaming while remembering her father and her life on the sea. Her savings were building up, piece by piece, and although she did not believe she would be able to buy a train ticket soon, she believed that she would one day.

Sometimes, on those walks, she found herself overcome with sadness and anger, and she had to sit by the river bank and look up at the clouds in the sky until calmness returned. She was angry with her father, she realised, even though he had done nothing to wrong her. She was angry that he had left her alone in this world, when he had promised to protect her and be there for her always. No one had ever wanted her, not Aunt Ida, not David, not anyone, except her papa, and in the end, he had left her too.

She did not like the thought, but she could not stop herself from feeling it. She hoped, desperately, that finally visiting his grave might bring her some peace. She could say goodbye to him properly, say all the things she had wished to say to him over the past four years, and then she thought her confused anger would settle, and she would be able to accept that he was gone.

CHAPTER FIFTEEN

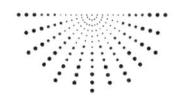

After another few months at the Cannings' house, Heather felt that politeness and propriety meant that she had to offer to leave, but again, Madge refused the suggestion straight away.

"I would miss you," she said. "And I know Trevor would miss you. He's grown quite fond of you, you know."

"He's fond of everybody," Heather said. "Except perhaps the capitalists," she added, as an afterthought.

"Well, he's *especially* fond of you. I hope I'm not too wild in hoping that you will officially join the family one day in the not too distant future."

Heather blushed. "Oh," she said. "I don't know. Trevor's never said anything."

"He hasn't said," Madge interrupted, "but he's been thinking it. I know he has. And you are so good together."

Heather found herself considering it as she tried to fall asleep that night. She knew that Trevor was a good person, and she enjoyed his company, but did she appreciate him that way, the way a woman would appreciate her future husband? He did not set butterflies off in her stomach or fill her heart with warmth with a simple smile, the way David had.

But then, David had forsaken her. The attachment between them had never been real. Perhaps, she thought, this was what real, lasting love was. Not a rush of feeling, but comfortable companionship.

Still, she thought, she could not get married yet. She still had so much to say to her father, so much grief she needed to have healed. Perhaps after she returned from Grimsby, and she was surprised to realise she was considering returning from Grimsby at all, she might be able to consider it.

In the meantime, she and Trevor continued their evening discussion over the newspaper, and he began inviting her for walks along the riverside. Each time, Heather would ask Madge if she wished to join them, and each time Madge would find an excuse to remain home, sending them off with a smile and a wink. She had to admit that Trevor was a good walking companion. He did not provide that same feeling of calm and acceptance that Heather had felt when she walked by David's side, but she had been young and naive then, wrapped up in a fantasy that could never come true. It made sense, she told herself, that things felt different now.

Outside the confines of the kitchen walls, Trevor grew even more passionate in his speech, sometimes raising his voice to the point that it made Heather jump. Every time this happened, he would pause and apologise, before continuing in a lower voice, reiterating the importance of whatever labour issue or political puzzle had got him so riled up in the first place.

Heather liked him. And perhaps, she thought, if he were one day to propose, after she had visited her father's grave, she might accept him. Perhaps this was what love and companionship was meant to be.

Besides, she often thought, when she was alone at night and the darkest thoughts crept into her mind, she had proved so difficult to love. Could she really afford to reject affection from anyone, when it was almost certain that no one else would ever show interest again?

Still, when Trevor cleared his throat on a walk one Saturday afternoon and told Heather that he had something important to discuss with her, Heather realised that all her thinking had been in vain, because she was not prepared for this discussion at all. She blushed scarlet as Trevor walked beside her, his hands clasped in front of him, looking at the path instead of her as he spoke.

"I hope, Miss Green, Heather, that I am not speaking out

of turn here, and that I am not mistaken that you are aware of and perhaps even welcome my affections."

"Out of turn?" Heather asked, with an awkward laugh. "When have you ever cared about that?"

"True," Trevor said. "But I don't want to upset you. I like to think that we have built a solid friendship these past few months. I know I have appreciated your company, more than you can know."

"I've appreciated you too," Heather said. That, at least, felt both safe and true to say.

"But you can't have missed how much I care for you," he said, "not just as a friend, but as a man cares for a woman, I suppose. I'm sorry. I'm not very good at this. It's hard to know what to say. Unusual for me, struggling for words, I know. But Heather, I rather hoped that perhaps you might return my affections," he said. "I hoped that perhaps you would agree to marry me. I know it would make my mother very happy, and of course me as well. Would it make you happy? Please say that it would."

Heather picked at a loose thread on the cuff of her dress as they walked, unable to look at him. She was feeling a rush of emotions, of gratitude, of affection, but most of all of panic, like a sheep hemmed in for the slaughter.

"Trevor," she said softly. What to address first? "I do appreciate your attentions," she said. "I have greatly enjoyed our evening conversations. You are one of the first people since my father to treat me like I might have an intellectual mind of my own, and I have appreciated that very much."

"But," Trevor said, sounding suddenly stern, "you are refusing me."

"No," Heather said quickly, the panic surging inside her. "It is not that, at all. It is just, I am not ready, Trevor. My life, my heart… I am not in a place where I can accept."

"Then what would it take," Trevor asked, "for you to accept me?"

"I plan to return home to Grimsby," Heather said, "as soon as I can afford the train fare there and back. I have not been there in many years, and not at all since my father died. I have not even visited his grave. I need to do that, I think. I need to see it, and to say goodbye to him there. I cannot move on with my life until that is done."

"Well, that is easy," Trevor said, sounding relieved. "We can get married, and in time we can save and make the journey together. It will be far easier with a husband beside you."

"No, Trevor," Heather said. "I cannot do that. This is something I need to do before I marry."

"It seems foolish," Trevor said, "to delay your own happiness in honour of someone who is gone. Surely you can make peace with his spirit from here, as easily as in front of his grave. The man is hardly tied to it."

"I know that," Heather said, feeling suddenly frustrated. Why was he not listening to her? "But it is something I need to do. I cannot think of marrying until I have done so. Please believe me, Trevor."

"Very well," Trevor said. "I understand. I do not want you to be unhappy."

"Thank you," Heather whispered.

"But I hope you know that you are making me very unhappy," he added.

Heather fought the urge to cry. "I am not saying no," she said, through her tears. "But I cannot say yes, not yet."

"See, and now you're crying," Trevor said. "You've upset yourself. Why don't we turn for home? I think mother has some coffee grinds in the cupboard. That should cheer you up."

Heather wiped her eyes with the back of her hand and nodded. "It really isn't no," she said. "Please understand."

"I understand, Heather," he said, sounding resigned. "Let's get you home."

Although Trevor claimed that he understood, he certainly acted as though he did not. He said a few quiet words to his mother that evening, and although Heather did not hear what they were, Madge's quiet embrace of her suggested that he had not told her he had been rejected. Life continued mostly as normal, but now Madge mentioned 'when you two are married' as a matter of course, and Trevor never corrected her. Considering the circumstances, Heather felt too awkward and unsure to correct her either. She had told Trevor maybe, hadn't she? Just not yet. She could not tell Madge that the future event she spoke of was not certain, when it seemed likely that it would happen one day, and certainly not after Madge had done so much for her.

In time, Trevor began to talk about their marriage like it was a set agreement as well. He spoke fiercely of the future he wanted to create for their children, and he would make casual comments about the possibility of them getting married at the chapel by the bridge, or how he wished they could afford for Heather to dress fashionably in white.

Heather gave up arguing the point with him. She had said it was likely, after all, and she was still saving for her visit to her father. It would not be long now before she would have the money together. Besides, it was good to feel wanted, even loved, to have someone fight for her with so much stubbornness. Wasn't it? She had been so lonely for so much of her life. Was she really in a position to reject Trevor's affection, when he offered it so freely and with so much assurance?

Soon, Trevor began to steal the occasional kiss, and although Heather's heart pounded with memories of Matthew on that day by the stairs, she forced herself to accept it with a smile. She was being silly, she thought, remembering Matthew now. Trevor was a good man. He would never hurt her. And if they were going to be married anyway, what harm could be done by a kiss?

CHAPTER SIXTEEN

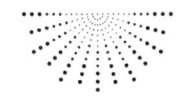

Eventually, the day came that Heather had saved enough money to buy her train ticket to Grimsby. She recounted the money again and again, just to be certain of the amount, but there was no mistake. All she needed to do was go to the railway station, and she would soon be reunited with her father again.

Madge embraced Heather when she told her, delighted that the day had finally come. "I'll miss you while you're gone," Madge said, "so make sure you hurry back, you hear me? I don't know what I'll do without you. I certainly don't know what Trevor will do without you."

"Oh, I'm sure he'll survive," Heather said. It was strange, but when she thought of Trevor now, her main feeling was relief. He would not be able to come to Grimsby with her. She would be able to spend the days without the pressure of his affection and discussions of their upcoming marriage. Of course, once she returned, the only impediment to their wedding would be over. And that was a good thing, Heather told herself. This is what she had wanted. She would find peace over her father's death, and then she would be able to move on.

When she told Trevor that evening, she had expected him to be similarly thrilled. Even if he thought her journey to Grimsby was silly and unnecessary, as she was certain he did, he would be delighted that their planning for their marriage could soon get truly underway. But he seemed somewhere between perplexed and furious when she told him she had finally saved up for the return fare.

"And you're going to take the train alone?" he asked her brusquely. "That doesn't sound safe. Mother or I should go with you."

"I only have enough for one," Heather said, "and this is a journey I really need to make alone."

"And where will you stay?" Trevor asked. "You can't sleep at your father's grave."

The question felt cruel, almost like he was mocking her, but Heather forced herself to stay calm. "My father owned the cottage we lived in," she said. "It was not rented. I will go there. And if it has gone to someone else, I have other friends in town. Someone will give me a floor to sleep on, I'm sure."

"A floor to sleep on," Trevor repeated, "or a house that no one has entered in years. This is your grand plan? You truly think your father's grave is worth it?"

"Yes," Heather said, feeling stung. "I do."

"Well, if you want to be a fool," Trevor muttered, "I can't stop you," and without another word, he strode from the room.

Heather blinked after him, and Madge shook her head. "Don't worry, dear," she said. "He's only worried about you, and he will miss you, like I will. It will all work out in the end." Heather was not so convinced, but she nodded anyway. Before she retired that night, she counted the money again, and then stuffed it into a sock to hide it at the bottom of her chest of clothes, just to be safe.

Trevor became increasingly snappy over the following days, and Heather began to think that it would be best if she took the trip as quickly as possible. She had hoped to leave during a slow time so that that her disappearance would not affect Madge or their sewing work, but the tenser Trevor got, the more desperate she became to take this chance, before she lost it somehow. She did not know what she feared, exactly, but she knew that fate could be a cruel thing, and people could be even crueller. She would not let this chance slip away.

Heather woke up early on the morning of her departure, and checked her bag and her money before heading downstairs. But as she stepped out into the upper hallway, she almost collided with Trevor.

"Oh, Trevor," she said. "I didn't see you there."

He took in the bag she was holding, and the neat way she'd pinned up her hair. "You're leaving," he said.

The statement almost sounded like a threat, but Heather forced herself to smile. "Yes," she said. "The first train to Grimsby. Well, the first train to Doncaster, and then on to Grimsby. " She shrugged. Trevor was not smiling. "I'll be back soon," she said. "A few days in Grimsby, and I'll be home before you know it."

"And if you don't?" Trevor asked. He was standing in such a way that Heather could not proceed to the stairs without pushing her way past him, so she stayed by the doorway, looking up at him.

"If I don't what?" she asked.

"If you don't come back," he prompted.

"I'm coming back," she said. "I have nothing left there now."

"Then why are you going at all?"

"I've told you," Heather said. "I need to see my father."

"Your father's grave," Trevor said. "Do you even know where it is? He died at sea, didn't he? He might not even have a grave."

"Well, then there'll be a plaque," Heather said. "There'll be something. Or I can just go to the docks where he tied his boat. I have to go, Trevor. I've told you this."

"I don't like it," Trevor said. "I told you I don't like it, and you're still insisting on going?"

"You don't own me, Trevor," Heather said softly. "You don't get to tell me what I can do."

"I as good as own you," Trevor said. "We'll be married soon, and then you'll have to listen to what I say. Or don't you have any respect for me at all?"

"We will not be married," Heather said, "if you insist on behaving like this. I am going to Grimsby, Trevor. That is final." She pushed her way past him towards the stairs, and Trevor grabbed her arm, squeezing hard enough to hurt. Heather's thoughts instantly flashed back to Matthew, the way he had grabbed her before he attacked her, and for a moment she forgot how to breathe. "Let go of me," she said.

"Not until you listen to me," Trevor said. "You said you were going to marry me. We've already agreed. So you need to listen to me."

"I said no such thing!" Heather said. "I never agreed to marry you. I told you that I needed to see my father first. But you haven't been listening to me."

"We were agreed," Trevor insisted. "We're engaged."

"We are not," Heather shouted. "And we never will be, if you don't let go of me right now." She wrenched her arm out of his grip and strode to the top of the stairs. Trevor hurried after her.

"Heather, I forbid it!"

"You can't forbid me anything," Heather said. "I would never marry a brute like you."

Trevor lashed out, striking her hard across the face. The force sent Heather stumbling backwards, and she tripped over the top step. She felt herself falling, her limbs striking the stairs as she went. When she collided with the floor, she knew no more.

CHAPTER SEVENTEEN

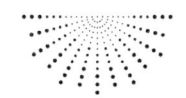

Madge had been listening to the entire thing from the bedroom, and upon hearing the crash, she rushed out, still in her night things. She took in the sight of her son standing at the top of the stairs, and Heather's crumpled body lying at the bottom, and she gasped.

"Trevor!" she said "What have you done?"

Trevor just stared at Heather's body, his mouth agape, saying nothing. Words seemed beyond him.

"Heather," Madge said, and she flew down the stairs after her. She lifted the unconscious girl's torso, placing her head upon her lap, and when she touched the back of the girl's skull, her fingers came away covered in blood. The girl was breathing, but only barely, and with that much blood, she could not possibly hang on for long. "You've killed her!" she shouted.

"I didn't mean to," Trevor said. "It was an accident."

"I know that," Madge said. "I know." Her Trevor would never hurt anybody on purpose, least of all Heather. He had just lost his temper. He had always been difficult when he could not get his own way. Perhaps that was Madge's fault, for indulging him. But what would become of him now, if it was discovered what had happened? He knocked her down the stairs. Would he be arrested for murder? Put in prison, or even hung for the crime?

Madge truly cared for Heather, and tears fell down her face as she looked at her ward and friend, but she could not let her son be arrested and possibly executed for an accident. He had not meant to do it, but if anyone found her here, if anyone knew what had happened to her…

"We have to move her," she said. "We can't leave her here."

"What are you suggesting?" Trevor asked. "We dump her in the canal?"

"No!" Madge said. She was feeling almost hysterical, but she needed to be calm, for Trevor's sake. She needed to think. "We'll take her to the hospital and leave her outside. Someone will find her there."

"She's dead, mother!" Trevor said, but Madge shook her head.

"She's not dead yet! She's dying, but she isn't dead. I won't dump her to die alone, or drown in the canal, for goodness sake! We'll take her to the hospital."

"What if someone sees us?" Trevor shouted.

"Then someone sees us!" Madge said. "Now quickly." She stood up and hurried to rinse the blood off her hands and then collect Heather's coat. It was still dark and cold outside, a grey November morning, and she wanted Heather to be comfortable. She could not get the girl's arms through the sleeves, so she draped it around her shoulders and buttoned it up at the front, before rushing to get her own coat and hat. "Pick her up, Trevor, for goodness sake," Madge said, and she heard her son's slow footsteps down the stairs. He swept Heather into his arms like she weighed nothing, and she hung limply there, like a rag doll.

"Why couldn't you control your temper?" Madge said. "Why couldn't you just let her go?"

"She threatened to leave me, Mother," Trevor said. "She said she wouldn't marry me."

"Well, she certainly won't be marrying you now!" Madge said. She felt on the edge of hysteria. "Come on with her. Quickly."

The pair carried Heather through the darkness, sticking to the quieter roads, and they met no-one. When they arrived at St. Mark Voluntary Hospital, gas lights burned outside the gate, and Madge could see lanterns through the windows inside. Doctors were working there, at least. But if they went up to the front door and knocked, everyone would know what her son had done.

"Leave her here," Madge said. "In front of the gate."

Trevor did as she said, depositing Heather onto the stone. His hands were stained with her blood.

Madge knelt in front of her friend and tucked a loose strand of hair behind her ear, away from her face. "I'm sorry," she said softly. "Please forgive me." She leant forward and kissed Heather on the forehead, and then stood, her vision blurred by tears. "Come on," she said to her son, and they hurried away into the darkness.

∽

Across Wakefield, Dr. David Armstrong was preparing for a day's work at the hospital. It was still early, but David was running slightly late, and his haste was making it even harder than normal to properly tie his cravat. It seemed ridiculous, he thought, as he adjusted it for the third time, that he needed to dress up so finely to head to the hospital, when he would only take the cravat off or risk it getting ruined once he arrived, but the wealthy patrons who sponsored the hospital insisted on many foolish things, and as long as they continued to donate their money, David supposed he could put up with far more nonsense than wearing a cravat.

Still, he felt more than a little rattled once he was finally ready to leave and hurried out of the door. The past couple of years had been good to David, and he had recently moved to a larger house a little outside

Wakefield, in a grassy, peaceful area called Heath. The little village offered a post office and a pub and a general store, and he knew it would be a good place to live once he got married and once his mother grew too old to live by herself in town, but it was also a good mile and a half outside of town, and David did not keep a carriage. Normally, he liked the walk, but when he was already running late, not so much. The autobus for the workers did not run at this hour, and the cab stands were empty.

As David strode towards town, his thoughts drifted again to the reason he was late. He had always been a punctual man, priding himself on his reliability, but he had been up past midnight the previous night, worrying about too many things. His mother was urging him to set a date for his wedding to Lauren, but David felt a reluctance that went far beyond what might be considered usual pre-wedding jitters. The fact was that he cared for Lauren, but he did not love her. Their relationship was driven by practicality and mutual respect, and not the heart. Their marriage made sense, but his doubts would not settle, and he had found himself unusually disturbed by them the previous night, unable to calm his racing thoughts and fall asleep.

When David finally approached St Mark's Voluntary Hospital, he was more than a little late and more than a little flustered, sweat from the exertion of the walk clinging to his brow despite the coolness of the morning.

He was so distracted, in fact, that at first he did not notice the figure lying abandoned before the hospital gates.

He was almost upon her when he spotted her, and for a moment he froze, unable to process what he saw. A young woman was sprawled out on the stone, a small pool of blood forming behind her head. She was wrapped in a worn dark woollen coat, and her blonde hair was falling out of a once neatly-pinned bun.

"Miss," he said. "Miss, are you alright?" What a foolish thing to say, he thought, as he bent down beside her. The woman was certainly not alright. He put a gentle hand on her arm and rolled her over until he could see her face. He gasped.

It was Heather Green.

CHAPTER EIGHTEEN

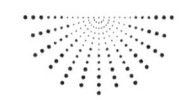

David had not seen Heather in almost a year. He had glanced her way occasionally when he visited her aunt, and she had always looked hurriedly away from him, until one day, even those sightings ended.

David had been horrified and heartbroken when Ida Owens first took him aside and warned him about her niece. She was a degenerate, Mrs. Owens had said gently, who grew up wild. She was found in a fishing boat as a child, and she had never quite learned the rules of society. Mrs. Owens did what she could to instil discipline and honour in the girl, but she remained a wild, manipulative thing, or so Mrs. Owens told him. She warned David, in as gentle terms as she could, that Heather was attempting to woo him for his money, and that she had several men about her, some rich to fund her, and some poor and uncouth and highly unsuitable society. Mrs. Owens confided in David that she feared Heather was attempting to trap David, in case her misbehaviour caught her in a delicate situation, and warned him not to be alone with her, if he could possibly avoid it.

Well, Mrs. Owens was a fussy, somewhat paranoid woman, but she was also an honourable one, well thought of by all Wakefield society, and David could not imagine that she would lie about something so serious. The younger Mrs. Owens had also made several distracted comments about Heather's behaviour that seemed to support the accusations, and David had quickly withdrawn, angry and more than a little hurt that he had been taken in by such a sweet and innocent-seeming girl's act.

When Heather had disappeared from the house entirely, David told himself he would not be deceived by her again, but he found himself a little worried about her absence. The Owens hired a maid, and it suddenly struck him that he had never seen one in the house before, despite the unlikelihood of either of the Mrs. Owens ever picking up a broom. He inquired about that, as well, asking how they liked their new maid and whether the previous one had left for fortuitous reasons, such as getting married, and Mrs. Owens informed him that there had been no previous maid, that Heather had kept the house clean and tidy but was no longer welcome, forcing them to spend money on additional help.

This struck David as strange. She had referred to Heather as both her niece and her ward, and had described her as partaking in many wild, time-consuming activities. It seemed odd that she would have time for such behaviour, and also single-handedly be able to keep the entire house as spotless as it had been. He commented that he hoped nothing terrible had befallen the young girl, and Mrs. Owens gave a put-upon sigh.

"She has just revealed her true colours," she said, "beyond any chance for doubt. I always had hope for her improvement, but it seems that blood and upbringing both win out, and what could I expect, really, from a little fisherwoman like her?"

"What happened?" David asked, trying to sound far less concerned than he truly was.

"The little viper tried to seduce my son," she said. "She then accused him of terrible, impossible things when she did not get her way. Well, it is all dealt with now. She is gone, and good riddance to her."

David had nodded and asked no further questions, but the thought of Heather continued to haunt him. He could not imagine the girl he knew behaving in such a way, but then, that had been what Mrs. Owens had told him, was it not? She was a talented actress and manipulator, and that she wanted the whole world to be under her thumb.

Yet Mrs. Owen's lack of concern for the girl's whereabouts or wellbeing seemed at odds with her previous statements regarding her niece, and David could not stop thinking about her. He began to listen for any gossip about the family, to steer conversations to her strange disappearance when he could, and on one visit to the house, he even headed down to the kitchen to try and talk to the cook about the matter.

This was where the truth came out. The Owens' cook was an elderly woman with little penchant for gossip, but her expression turned severe when David mentioned Heather, and she clucked her tongue and shook her head in disapproval.

"A bad business, that," she said. "I shouldn't speak ill of the family, but I felt sorry for the poor girl."

"Why?" David asked.

"Working in that factory for no pay, cleaning the house like a maid without a penny paid for that either, not a moment to herself and no food to eat if the work was not done to the mistress's satisfaction. It was a bad business, and I did what I could, but I couldn't go against the mistress's orders. And then of course there was that business with the master."

"What business is that?" David asked.

"I don't like to gossip," the cook said, "but it was terrible, truly it was. The young master has always had something of a wandering eye, and the girl grew up so pretty that of course she caught his attention. One afternoon, he thought he was in the house alone with her. No one ever thinks of the cook's presence, do they? Well, I heard the girl scream, and the master yell, and something of a struggle. My old knees can't carry me very fast these days, but I was about to run up the stairs, when I heard the mistress and Mrs. Edna arrive home. The shouting was terrible. The girl was crying, saying the young master had assaulted her, but the master denied it, and the mistress threw her out of the house. But you couldn't fake a scream like that. The poor girl was terrified, and the master's shouting was certainly terrifying to hear. I saw her leaving, too, all bruised with her dress torn. The poor girl. It was a bad business all around."

David stared at the cook in horror. How could he not have seen it? Heather had suffered under such abuse, and he had believed that she had been the wicked one. Along with sheer horror and despair at what had happened to her, he also felt a deep stirring of shame within him. He had believed Mrs. Owen's accusations against the evidence before his own eyes, and now Heather was gone, alone and who knew where.

When he climbed the stairs back to the main hallway, he saw Matthew Owens entering through the front door, and rage overtook him. He pulled his arm back and punched the man right in the face. The man recoiled and swore, and it took all of David's self-restraint not to strike him again. He heard the women yelling from the top of the stairs, but he ignored them, striding from the house and determined to never return.

He spent the next several weeks trying to find Heather. He checked the workhouse repeatedly, and the hospital. He spoke to the police, and he went to the foremen of several factories to ask them if any new young women had recently signed on to work. Yet there was nothing. He could not find a single sign of her. His only comfort was that, if she had died, the police would surely have known and made the connection, with the number of times he had inquired after her. But the fact remained that he could not find her. Heather Green seemed to have disappeared off the face of the earth.

Eventually, David was forced to slow his search. "I know you feel guilty, David, dear," his mother told him, "but you have other things to worry about. Your patients need you, and Lauren needs you too. You cannot seem so preoccupied by this girl, when you are engaged to another."

David had not wanted to abandon Heather, but his mother had been right. It was pointless, and it would hurt his engagement if Lauren knew. Although he did not feel the same way about Lauren that he did about Heather, he owed respect and kindness to her too.

And so David stopped his search for Heather, although he never stopped wondering what had become of her, until one November morning, when she fell back into his life, bleeding, unconscious, but alive, as though fate itself had finally seen fit to intervene.

CHAPTER NINETEEN

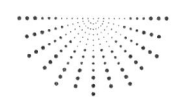

David swept Heather up into his arms and checked her breathing and her pulse. Her breathing was shallow, and her heartbeat was worryingly weak, but she was alive, and that at least was something. She lay limp in his arms like a rag doll as he ran through the gates and into the hospital, shouting for someone to prepare the operating room at once.

The wound on her head needed several stitches, but it was not as severe as the amount of blood had first suggested. Heather had a broken arm as well, and bruises on her back and around her ribs, and the doctors worked hard to fix what they could and make her comfortable for the rest to heal. Her injuries suggested she had taken a fall, a nasty one, and it seemed sheer luck that she was still alive at all.

Once they had done everything they could for her, David had her placed in a private room, small but clean, with sunlight streaming in through the window. He had dealt with all the injuries that he could see. Only time would tell whether the fall and the head wound had had any deeper, more permanent impact on her brain.

David was surprised and relieved to see that Heather looked otherwise healthy. She was a little pale, but she was well-fed, and she had no illness or apparent injuries other than those that must have occurred in the fall. Wherever she had been these past months, she could not have been destitute.

She could not have brought herself to the hospital gates alone. Her coat had been wrapped around her in such a way that suggested someone else had put it on her, and the size of her head wound and damage to her body would have made it almost impossible for her to stagger through the streets by herself. Someone had been taking care of her before the fall, David surmised, and had carried her to the hospital afterwards in hope of getting her some help. But if she had friends who would do that for her, why had they not brought her into the hospital proper, or at least left her at the front door instead of outside the gates?

Perhaps, he thought, it had not been a fall at all. But why would someone hurt her, and then bring her to the hospital? Had it been an accident, then?"

David had other patients that he had to attend to, but he returned to Heather as often as he could. She drifted in and out of consciousness, but she remained incoherent, murmuring to herself and tossing and turning on the bed. Multiple times, she called out for her papa, and David's heart ached for her, knowing that her father was long dead.

Heather would respond to no one, not even to him. Whenever she acknowledged someone's voice, it was only to ask them where her papa was, and whether he would be coming soon. She murmured to herself about having failed him, and cried that she was sorry.

It broke David's heart to see her, but she would respond to no one. As the days passed, he began to worry that her greatest injury was not physical, but deep in her thoughts and in her heart. She desperately needed her father, and, as he had seen when he had first met her, years before, his absence had taken her will to live.

David knew that contacting her aunt would do nothing to help her. Even if Ida Owens knew anything useful about Heather, he could not trust her to share it honestly, but he knew he had to do something to help her. Unless something changed, he knew she was likely to die, and he would be at least partly responsible for that. He had not harmed her directly, and he had done all he could to save her, but he had believed her aunt's lies about her character, and he had abandoned her to face that abuse alone.

David could not leave Heather or his other patients to head to Grimsby himself, but he had a family friend, an old acquaintance of his father named Frederick Smith, who had worked in Scotland Yard in London for many years before returning home to Wakefield to retire. The man had not taken to retired life as well as one might have hoped, however, and he always seemed eager to get back on the case, although these days his skills were restricted to novels and stories reported on in the newspaper.

David offered the man a fair sum of money to travel to Grimsby and enquire after the origins of Heather Green, a fisherman's daughter who rumour said had been left abandoned in the man's boat as a young child. Green was a common surname, and Heather was in no state to provide David with her father's Christian name, but Mr. Smith revelled in the idea of a challenge, and David hoped that the unusual nature of her story might make her easier to pin down. Mr. Smith was to learn as much as he could about the girl's past, find out exactly what happened to her father, and, if he found any other living relatives, to convince them to return to Wakefield with him in hopes of cheering the girl back to consciousness.

David had little hope in the plan's success, but what else could he do? He waited restlessly, while Heather continued in her delirium, on the edge of death. He was surprised, therefore, when Mr. Smith returned not three days later, with a worn looking man in tow.

"Not a bad job," Mr Smith said, "if I do say so myself. Dr. Armstrong, may I present to you Ambrose Green, Miss Green's father."

CHAPTER TWENTY

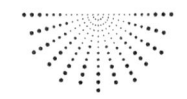

"Where is she?" the man claiming to be Heather's father asked. "Where's my daughter?"

David just stared at them. "Miss Green's father is dead," he said.

"Apparently not," Mr Smith said. "I found him in Grimsby, like you said. Everyone directed me to him when I asked about Miss Heather Green, and when he heard I had news about his daughter, he was frantically desperate to leave Grimsby and find her if he could."

David took in the stranger's appearance. He seemed to be in his fifties, but he still looked strong, with arm muscles that could only come from a lifetime of labour. His skin was weathered by the sun and the sea air, and his hair was salt and pepper, brown and grey. He wore a beard on his face, and he was looking around frantically, searching for Heather.

"Miss Green is here," David said to him gently. "And she is safe, although her condition is serious. But I confess myself at a loss, Mr. Green. Your daughter told me her father died several years ago in an accident at sea. I'm afraid I cannot allow you to see her, and possibly increase her distress, until I understand what is going on."

"I'm not dead," the man said bluntly. "I don't know why she would think that."

"Her aunt informed her," David said. "At least four years ago now. But if you are not dead, why didn't you contact her in all these years?"

"I tried to," David said. "I can't write, but I had a friend help me. At first, I received notes from her aunt, talking about her progress, but then they stopped. So I sent a letter enquiring after her, and almost a month later, I get a reply that my friends tells me says that my daughter has run off with a man, and her whereabouts are unknown. Her aunt was very angry. I hoped and hoped she'd come back to Grimsby one day, but I had no hope of finding her, when she could be anywhere in England. Then this gentleman shows up and tells me that she's been in Wakefield all along, and now she's injured, and a young doctor is inquiring after her family."

"It seems," David said heavily, "that her aunt has deceived

all of us. For what reason, I could not say. But Heather certainly did not leave years ago."

"And what is it to you?" Ambrose asked, looking David up and down. "How do you know my daughter?" He sounded almost accusing.

"Her aunt called on my assistance after she was informed of your death," he said. "She was drowning in her grief. Afterwards, I became a friend of the family, and grew to care for Heather very much, though I have not seen her since she went missing."

"Heather, is it?" Ambrose said. "Missing *where?*"

"I don't know, sir," David said. "There was an incident at her aunt's house. She suffered cruelty at the hands of her relatives, and I believe she fled. I had been searching for her, to no avail, until several days ago, when someone left her in front of the hospital gates. She seemed to have suffered some accident or fall. I must inform you, Mr. Green, that her condition is severe."

"Will she live?" Ambrose asked.

"I don't know, sir," David said. "It seems unlikely. But she has been calling for you constantly. I sent Mr. Smith to Grimsby to see if he might find some living relative, or some useful information to bring back, to help sooth her and maybe bring about a change in her condition."

"Then show me to her," Ambrose said. "I have to see her."

David nodded and led the man through the hospital to Heather's room. Heather was asleep, her head turned to one side, blonde hair spilling on the pillow around her like a halo. One arm was bent above the blankets, revealing the bruises there.

Ambrose gasped when he saw her, and hurried across the room to her side. "Heather," he said. "My Heather." He took her hand in his, squeezing tightly, tears in his eyes. "I'm sorry," he whispered. "I'm sorry I sent you away, Heather. I'm sorry I trusted in that woman, and left you to suffer here alone. Please wake up, my girl. Wake up, and let me see your smile again. Wake up, and forgive me."

Heather stirred. David sprang forward as she shifted her head, murmuring softly, but he managed to restrain himself from getting too close. Her father leaned closer to her, squeezing her hand fiercely. "That's it, Heather," he said. "Wake up, now. It's all going to be alright. I'm here, you see. I'm here, and I'll never be parted from you again. I just need you to wake up."

Heather's eyelids fluttered. "Papa?" she murmured.

"Yes, Heather," her father said. "I'm here."

∾

Heather felt as though she were dreaming. Her arms and legs felt heavy, and her thoughts were hazy beneath a pounding headache, but in the distance, she could have sworn she heard her father's voice. She must have been dreaming, because that was impossible. Her papa was dead, and she had failed him. No one cared for her now.

Still, the voice that sounded like papa continued to call to her, begging her to wake. *I don't want to*, she thought vaguely. *I want to stay dreaming, where you can be with me.* She felt somebody squeezing her hand. Strange, that a dream could do such things.

She shifted, and the voice grew louder, more insistent. She tried to reach towards it, desperate for a glimpse of her papa, even if it was only a dream, but the world was dark around her, and she could not see. She tried to blink, to clear her vision, and that was when she realised her eyes were closed. She dragged them open.

The light of the room was too bright, and she blinked several times, while the man before her gasped. "Papa?" she murmured. He couldn't really be here. Was she dead, then? The last thing she remembered was arguing with Trevor, him striking her and the air rushing around her as she fell. It felt like it had happened so long ago. Had she been reunited with her father at last?

She blinked again, squeezing his hand back, surprised by how solid it felt. He was certainly no ghost or spirit. Behind him, she saw David and a man she did not know, both staring at her in wonder. That did not make sense either, she thought. David was not dead, but her father was not alive.

"What happened?" she murmured.

"You had an accident," her papa said. "Dr. Armstrong found you. We thought you had died, Heather."

"I'm not dead?" she asked. Her throat felt raw.

"No, my love," her papa said. "You're not dead."

She blinked again, trying to make her thoughts make sense. "But you're dead," she said. "Aunt Ida told me. She said you died at sea.."

"Your Aunt Ida lied to you," her father said. "She lied to me to, or I would have found you long before. I told you I'd see you again, didn't I? And I keep my promises."

"Papa," she murmured.

"Rest now," her father said. "You've been through so much."

"Don't leave, Papa," she said, and he shook his head as her eyes fluttered closed again.

"I won't," he said. "I promise. I won't ever leave your side again."

CHAPTER TWENTY-ONE

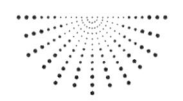

Heather's recovery was slow, but gradually, her condition improved. Her father stayed beside her day and night, speaking soothing words to her, telling her stories and memories of the sea. When Heather was awake enough to sit up, she told her father and David what had happened to her. David did not know whether he was angrier at her aunt or at the man who had knocked her down the stairs, but Heather became agitated if he was agitated, so he forced himself to remain calm as she talked.

At least, he thought, this Madge Canning had been friend enough to bring her to the hospital, even if she had not been good enough to bring her inside.

David was desperate to speak to Heather alone. He needed to apologise to her for all that had happened, and for believing such terrible lies about her, but her father remained true to his word, and he never left her side, forcing David to continue to play the caring doctor and nothing more.

Heather, for her part, was confused by David's presence. He told her how he had found her outside the hospital, so she understood that, at least, but every time David looked at her now, he did so with affection and warmth. He stared at her sometimes like she was a marvel, like the very fact that she was alive was a blessing, and Heather supposed it was a miracle, considering what David had told her. What she did not understand was *why* he seemed so affected. The last time she had seen him, he had hated her. Could his opinion truly have changed that much?

David, meanwhile, was struggling with his own feelings. His fiancé became frustrated by his constant work, and he was eventually forced to admit to her that an old friend had been taken gravely ill, and he was spending as much time with her as he could. Far from being angry or suspicious, Lauren expressed her sincere sympathies, and insisted that she come and visit the hospital at once, to offer her support to the invalid and to help keep her fiancé company. The goodness inherent in that impulse caused David great pain. This was a woman, he knew, who deserved to be fully appreciated for all the wonderful qualities she possessed. She did not deserve to be married to a man who may one day grow to resent her, because she was herself and not someone else.

David quietly broke off the engagement, and Lauren gave him a knowing glance as he spoke to her, but nodded without any tears, and said that she understood.

If the rest of Heather's so-called family heard about her illness, they certainly did not care enough to call at the hospital and check that she was alive. David was almost glad of it. He did not think he would be able to keep calm in their presence. Once Heather was well enough to talk to the police, he had them interview her about the assault. They seemed sceptical of Heather's story, considering she had been living with the family, including a young man, despite there being no relation between them, and David was furious in her defence, demanding that justice had to be done.

Heather cried, and said that she did not want Madge to come to any harm, but she did not mention Trevor, and so David continued to push for prosecution. Yet when the police visited the Cannings' home, Trevor was gone. His tearful mother said he had been missing for several days with no explanation, but that most of his clothes and all of his money had gone with him, so he must have chosen to leave. When the police told her that Heather was alive, she sobbed from both heartbreak and relief, understanding now why her son had fled and horrified by all that had occurred.

Through David, Heather invited Madge to visit her in the hospital, and although David did not agree that it was a good idea, he could not bear to deny her. Madge sat by her bedside for an hour, crying and apologising, while Heather insisted on thanking her for all the care she had given her, and for doing the right thing by taking her to the hospital, even though she seemed certain to die.

"I would not be alive without you," Heather said softly. "I would have died twice over if you hadn't been there. I cannot forget that, Madge."

Madge sobbed, and she swore that Heather was the sweetest heart she had ever known. Once she had gone, Heather commented that she did not think it wise to keep up the acquaintance, but that she could not regret having met her, as she had kept her alive and brought her father back into her life.

Heather glanced at David as she said this, and David had the sudden thought that Heather was thankful that he had been brought back into her life too, but he did not dare question her about it, especially in front of her father.

Once Heather recovered enough to leave the hospital, the question arose as to where she would go to finish her recuperation. Both Aunt Ida and Madge's houses were obviously out of the question, and David did not think she was capable of the long train journey to Grimsby to her childhood home.

"You must stay with me," he said. "You and your father both. My house is more than large enough, and that way I can provide any additional care you may require."

Ambrose gave David an appraising look, but then he nodded, and agreed that it was a solid idea. Heather frowned at him in confusion, but she did not contradict her father.

Later that day, when Ambrose had fallen asleep in the chair by Heather's bedside, Heather turned to David.

"Is it truly all right for us to stay with you?" she asked tentatively.

"Of course," David said. "I insist on it."

"Will your fiancé not mind?" she asked.

David shook his head. "We broke off our engagement," he said.

"Oh," Heather said. "I'm sorry to hear that."

"It was for the best," David said. "She was a wonderful girl, but she could never be first in my affection."

"Oh," Heather said, and she blushed. "I see. Well, then. I would very much like to accept your offer. If it is still available."

Two days later, Heather and her father moved into chambers in David's country house. David still had to leave often to work at the hospital and run his practice, but he saw Heather at least once a day, and he delighted in her curiosity as she grew stronger. She told him again how her father had wished her to come to Wakefield for an education, and he offered her anything in his library that she might desire to read. She devoured everything after that, reading to and teaching her father as she went. She read travelogues and political treatises, histories and medical books, and David laughed in delight when he returned from work one day to find Heather eager to take his hand and name every bone in it from memory. Heather was so clinical and methodical in her work that she did not seem to realise she was holding his hand, touching him skin to skin, until she had finished her work, and then she blushed, but she did not let go.

David desperately wanted to ask her to marry him, but after hearing her story about what had happened with Trevor Canning, he was loathe to make her feel pressured again in any way. In the meantime, he tried to just enjoy her company, and support her, whatever she decided for the future.

It was a few months later, when he and Heather were sitting in the garden on a Sunday afternoon, each with their own book in their laps and lost in their own thoughts, when he noticed Heather looking at him rather strangely.

"Is everything all right?" he asked her, and she nodded slowly and distractedly.

"I'm merely wondering," she said, "if you ever plan to ask me to marry you. I thought perhaps that was your intention, when you first invited me here, although I should not make assumptions. But you told me that there was another woman you preferred over Lauren Thompson, and I hoped-- but you have said nothing since then, and I would rather know, instead of wondering about it. Do you care for me, David? Do you wish to marry me?"

"I care for you very much," David said, springing to his feet and hurrying towards her. "And I would very much like to have you as my wife, if you will have me."

Heather smiled, and her entire face lit up with the joy in it.

"I'm sorry I did not say anything before," David said. "I was not certain how you felt. But yes. Please be my wife. Please marry me."

"I will," Heather said. "You silly man. How could you ever think I might want anything or anyone but you?"

David kissed her.

CHAPTER TWENTY-TWO

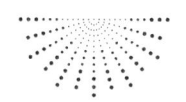

Heather and David were married on a bright April morning, not two weeks after their mutual proposal. Heather cried tears of joy as her father walked her down the aisle, and David thought that there had never been a more beautiful vision in the world than the sight of his love in her wedding dress. They said their vows before a small audience of friends, and David's mother exclaimed how well the two of them looked together, and how happy she was to welcome Heather into the family.

"He comes to life when you're around," she confided in Heather that day. "I've never seen such joy for life in him. I'm proud to call you my daughter, my dear."

Upon hearing these words, Heather cried again, overwhelmed by the love around her. A few months before, she had felt like she had no one who truly loved her, and now had an entire family. And after all she, David, and her father had been through, she knew they would not be pulled apart easily again, not even if all the world schemed against them.

The wedding day came with one surprise. Aunt Ida, Matthew, and Edna had heard about David's upcoming nuptials to a Miss Lauren Thompson, and when they learned of a date set for the wedding and a celebration on the green in Heath afterwards, they naturally assumed that this was the union taking place. Aunt Ida felt snubbed by her lack of direct invitation, and as the celebration afterwards was technically public, she decided that she and her family simply must attend. It would not do for Wakefield society to think that the Owens had been excluded on purpose, and Aunt Ida hoped that their mere presence would be rebuke enough for the doctor's carelessness.

Words could not describe Aunt Ida's shock and horror when the family arrived at Heath to find her niece arm in arm with Dr. Armstrong, smiling broadly with flowers woven in her hair. Aunt Ida had long ago dismissed Heather for dead, or at the very least lost to both society and morality, and she was momentarily left speechless as she gaped at the scene. Then she saw Ambrose smiling at his daughter, and her heart stopped. All of her lies and deception unravelled before her eyes, and she could suddenly imagine what would happen to her and her family if Ambrose or Dr. Armstrong chose to confront them here. Their reputation would be ruined, and perhaps their business with it too. Aunt Ida might never be able to show her face in company again.

Aunt Ida let out a gasp and clutched at her chest as her second heart struck her. The newlyweds looked up at the sound, and one of the many doctors in attendance was soon by her side and helping to convey her to the very hospital that had saved Heather not long ago.

Yet, as marvellous as modern medicine was, there was little that it could do to repair the shock brought to a wicked heart by the failure and illumination of all its ill deeds. Aunt Ida was dead by morning, and although Heather had not wanted her wedding day to be memorable in society for the death of a well-known woman, she could not mourn the loss.

Matthew and Edna, for their part, struggled to survive without Aunt Ida's iron will upon them. It soon came out that Matthew had been embezzling funds from the factory, and he fled the city, only to be captured and arrested and put in prison for several years. Edna, seeing the imminent collapse of the factory, stole what was left of the money and ran away with one of the workers, leaving the mill to collapse in their absence.

Heather worried for the well-being of those who had worked in the factory, but the unstoppable drive of progress provided plenty of jobs in the endless new factories and mills that opened, and although Heather was never friendly with Madge again, she was pleased to hear that her mending, and later her tailoring, business was more than enough to keep her well.

Ambrose was true to his word, and stayed by Heather's side for all the rest of his days. They kept the cottage and the fishing boat in Grimsby, and Heather and her father made frequent trips to the village, where they got hot drinks from Mrs. Atha's stall, chatted with people in the market, and took the boat out into the sea. Surrounded by blue waves and open sky, they made up for all the years they had lost. David travelled to Grimsby too, when his work allowed him to, and Heather delighted to see the man slightly out of his element on the waves. One day, David promised, he would move his practice and they would retire to the coast, but now, Heather had grown to love Wakefield. It was the place where she met David, after all.

Heather and David had their disagreements over the years, as all couples do, but their relationship was strengthened by all the hardship they had undergone to come together, and they always felt secure in their love. Nothing could ever cause them to part from one another, and they lived happily together for the rest of their days.

THANK YOU FOR CHOOSING A PUREREAD BOOK!

We hope you enjoyed the story, and as a way to thank you for choosing PureRead we'd like to send you this free book, and other fun reader rewards...

Click here for your free copy of Whitechapel Waif
PureRead.com/victorian

Thanks again for reading.
See you soon!

LOVE VICTORIAN ROMANCE?

If you enjoyed this story why not continue straight away with other books in our PureRead Victorian Romance library?

Read them all...

Orphan Christmas Miracle

An Orphan's Escape

The Lowly Maiden's Loyalty

Ruby of the Slums

The Dancing Orphan's Second Chance

Cotton Girl Orphan & The Stolen Man

Victorian Slum Girl's Dream

The Lost Orphan of Cheapside

Dora's Workhouse Child

Saltwick River Orphan

Workhouse Girl and The Veiled Lady

OUR GIFT TO YOU

AS A WAY TO SAY THANK YOU WE WOULD LOVE TO SEND YOU THIS BEAUTIFUL STORY FREE OF CHARGE.

Our Reader List is 100% FREE

Click here for your free copy of Whitechapel Waif

PureRead.com/victorian

At PureRead we publish books you can trust. Great tales without smut or swearing, but with all of the mystery and romance you expect from a great story.

Be the first to know when we release new books, take part in our fun competitions, and get surprise free books in your inbox by signing up to our Reader list.

As a thank you you'll receive an exclusive copy of Whitechapel Waif - a beautiful book available only to our subscribers...

Click here for your free copy of Whitechapel Waif

PureRead.com/victorian

Printed in Great Britain
by Amazon